In The Shadows Of The Pines

Thirteen Mysterious Tales From The Old North State

Joe Sledge

Books by Joe Sledge

Did You See That? A Travel Guide To North Carolina's Out
Of The Ordinary Attractions

Did You See That? On The Outer Banks

Did You See That? Too!

Did You See That Ghost?

Haunting The Outer Banks

Bess Truly And Her Zap-Gun Rangers

The Unmerciful Sea (as John Martell)

Nag's Head: Or, Two Months Among The Bankers (editor,
author of appendixes)

In the Shadows Of The Pines

Joe Sledge

Copyright © Joe Sledge/Gravity Well Books 2021
ISBN-978-0-9980968-8-9
First paperback edition 2021

Published by Gravity Well Books

This one's for my father.

That guy could really tell a story.

Table Of Contents

Introduction

This Haunted Land is truly a well earned description for North Carolina. Ghost tale readers will easily recognize the title of the iconic book by Nancy and Bruce Roberts, which collected and told the spooky stories that we then retold and reread time and time over. From the ocean to the mountains, every old house, old bridge, tangled forest, falling down barn, and any deep set shadow held the  legend of a ghost or haunt within it, ready to be told to kids and adults alike.

We love those stories. They are still read, late at night, hoping for a blood curdling good time. The tales of ghosts across The Old North State have been recorded, told, embellished, and dramatized. Parents and older siblings tell them to scare the little ones, who then try their best to repeat them, to scare the next person with the same story that scared them.

Some are so well told that they have become popular chestnuts, to the point that we no longer tell the tale, just the ending. "She's just trying to get home," ends the story of Lydia, the poor girl abandoned at the bridge in Jamestown in the rain, a ghostly hitchhiker looking for a ride. Or "O, cry, cock!" belted out by Blackbeard's detached head as it swam around the boat near Ocracoke Inlet. Yes, we know them well.

So I hunted for tales less known. I wanted something, well, if not new, then at least tales untold. I think I found a good collection. A few of these tales appear in other books, but others are very obscure. Some are more accurate to the truth, whatever that might be when dealing with ghostly legends and the supernatural, and supply a bit more color to a simple old tale. Others take a slightly more liberal approach to a haunt. You may choose to believe what you want. You may be entertained, or you may be chilled, even terrified.

Then, after reading, keep the stories alive. As Nancy Roberts said in her book, remember those who came before you. North Carolina is truly a haunted land, its history comes alive. It crosses from the past to the present. Those spirits, the lost souls, the soldiers, colonists, and natives to the land, the spooks still clinging to this world, they could be right next to you. Share their stories. Go work up a good scare!

The Lights of Earley Station

July 10, 1968
Rich Square

The summer heat rolled in hard by July. Throughout the small town of Rich Square, the sun beat down on everything. Workers sweltered in the heat. Even the hardy peanut and tobacco plants drooped in the midday sun. Kids sought out any shade or cool spot around the old houses that circled the old downtown. It was too hot to even walk into town to get a drink from the drugstore. The heat would melt the ice in any cup before they could get back to their houses.

Two young boys, Johnny, nearing nine years old in the next week, and his brother Robert, just turned eight last month, basking in the short time he was his older brother's equal, lay in deep clover that grew under the cover of a tall oak tree. Each nursed a bottle of Coca-Cola, with the small green glass growing slippery moment by moment as condensation formed on the outside of the bottle. They drank slow enough to make the Coke last, but not so slow that the drink got warm and ruined the wonderful cool burn they tasted with every sip. The two had escaped their grandparents' house to sit quietly in the shade. Everyone else was inside, cooing over their new baby brother that they had already seen every day for months. The gentle buzz of insects and the cloying scent of the green clover was a welcome respite. It was worth the heat to get away, even for a moment.

That was why, a few hours later, they jumped at a chance to go on an adventure with the next door neighbor. Raymond had seen the two boys, bored and lounging in the backyard, and realized they would both enjoy a trip out exploring, as well as make good marks for a little joke.

"Hey, you fellas want to go see a ghost?"

That's all it had taken, so after a quick dinner, the two kids found themselves bouncing along in Raymond's old pickup truck, heading toward Ahoskie. Johnny sat on the passenger side, hanging his head out the window, letting the summer wind blow into his face and eyes until he began to tear up. Robert, being younger, suffered in the middle of the big vinyl bench seat with the warm blowing air of the vents on him. To compensate for him sitting on the hump, Raymond let Robert shift the gears on the column of the truck. The smells of tobacco smoke, red dirt, gas and antifreeze all permeated the cab of the old truck. The scents were as familiar to the boys as the green clover and ivy that grew around their grandparents' house.

"What ghost are we going to see?" asked Robert. Johnny pulled his head in to listen.

Raymond dangled one arm out the open window. The other rested lazily on the steering wheel. He waited a moment to build up the suspense. "Weeellll...." he said.

"There was this train conductor, see? Named James Pearce. He ran a freight train up the line toward Ahoskie," Raymond pointed ahead. It was a soft gesture that went well with the soft earthy twang that graced the language of the locals of the region. "He was going up the line, toward Aulander over there, toward Earley Station, down near Ahoskie. He saw another train comin' up the line, on the same line, see? But in the opposite direction.

"So, he put on the brakes and tried to slow his train down. But that didn't work well." At that moment, Raymond tapped the brakes of his old truck. Everyone lurched forward and flopped back into the bench seat. "Try to stop a big heavy train fast. Just can't do it. He slowed down some, but that other train just kept comin' on. James braced for the crash. But nothing happened. The train comin' at him just vanished. It was a phantom."

"So, is that what we're gonna see, a ghost train?" Johnny asked. The boys tried to act excited, but Raymond could already see they were getting nervous.

"Naw. You gotta hear the rest of the story." Raymond knew he had them now. "See, James stopped at Earley Station to report the train going the other way. But there was no train, and the boys at the station started teasing him for making it all up. 'Cause he was runnin' late. So James Pearce just slammed the pen down, stopped writing the report, and got on to his train.

"After he got going, the train derailed a few miles down the line, and James Pearce was killed." Raymond paused, again, to get the kids full attention. "Now, as soon as it gets dark, you go out down at Earley Station and look down the railroad. You can see a light appear over the track. They say it's James Pearce. He's trying to get back to write that report. If he had only done that, he might have saved his life."
Johnny and Robert looked at each other, wide-eyed. The two giggled and beat the big bench seat in their excitement.

"Now, hang on for a minute, okay, boys?" Raymond said as he pulled into a gravel parking lot. There was a small store just off the road, selling local produce picked from the nearby fields, along with the sundries that the residents needed. The store advertised cold drinks and beer, along with snacks and treats, cupcakes and candies. A big homemade sign read "Henry's" above the door. "I just gotta go in here and get a pack of cigarettes."

Raymond went inside, leaving the boys to wait in fear and anticipation of what would happen next. They each coped with their fright in different ways. Robert teased his brother, "I bet you'll jump out of your shoes!"

Johnny, the older brother, and by default having to be the braver one, said nothing back. He tried to be unmoved by the taunt.

Raymond came back only minutes later. "Let's get going, boys. It's getting dark now. Don't want to miss it."

They drove down the small two lane road, toward Earley Station. The old building was standing, but empty and leaning. Raymond pulled his truck into the dusty clay parking lot. Pulling an old chrome flashlight from the glove compartment, he told the boys, "Now, you be careful gettin' out. There could be a real train on those tracks."

He shone the flashlight onto the ground as they walked up to the crossroads where the tracks and road met. They stood just to one side of the tracks, under the silent and unlit lights and bell that warned of passing trains. The air was warm, still, and thick, full of the dirt and dust that permeated the summer all around the county. The smell of creosote and oil hung in the air around the tracks. Raymond shone his flashlight down the track. "Now, you boys just watch down the track. Soon enough, you'll see old Jame Pearce himself appear, wavin' his signal lamp, tryin' to get back to this here station." Then he turned his light off.

The three of them waited. It was fully dark now, and the sky was an inky black, dotted with stars on a cloudless night. Their eyes adjusted to the darkness. Nothing happened for a full minute. Johnny could hear Robert open and close his mouth, trying to say something, but not wanting to be the first one to break the silence and the magic.

Then, far down along the side of the tracks, a faint glow appeared. A yellow light, bright and round, wobbled up onto the tracks. "See? See it, boys? There it is. That's Earley Light!

7

That's old James Pearce himself!" Raymond was delighted with himself.

"Wow..." Johnny sighed out a soft recognition. It was the first time he had ever seen a ghost. Robert said nothing, but shuffled closer to Raymond.

The light made its way up the side of the tracks and began a soft bouncy march along the tracks. It was probably a mile away, or it could have been only a hundred yards. They boys had no idea how close it was. They were thrilled and terrified at the same time.

"Is it... is he... does he keep coming down the tracks?" Robert finally asked.

"Yup," Raymond answered. "He's heading right here. Right to that building there. Maybe we'll be lucky and he'll make it this time." Even in the dark, there was no disguising the smile in Raymond's voice.

"What do we do if he gets here?" Robert asked with a hint of fear in his voice.

Johnny, scared too, but also intrigued, grabbed at his brother. "He's coming for you! We'll leave you here for him!"

"Don't worry, boys, he never makes it. The light always goes out long down the line." Fun was fun. Raymond wanted to give them a little scare, but he didn't want the kids to have nightmares. "See? It's already moving off."

The light dipped, and then moved to one side. Then it began moving back down the line again, toward the three of them. From behind the light, another glow appeared in the thick trees that lined the railroad. It moved up the side of the tracks. It started following the first light down the rails.

"Are there supposed to be two lights?" Johnny finally spoke.

Raymond answered tersely. "I ain't never seen that before, boys." He stared, quiet, down the straight rail line. Then he knelt down and felt the cold, still rails.

The first light moved closer, and faster. But the second light began to glow brighter. It grew to a bright white, far outdoing the dim luminescence of the first light's yellow glow. The bright white orb bounded in wide loops up the track, while the yellow light bounced erratically, as if it were skipping and tripping across the wooden ties.

For a fleeting moment, Johnny and Robert could see both lights, one in front of the other, as well as an indistinct outline of a human form. "It's him! It's the conductor!" Robert screamed. He grabbed at Raymond's pants leg.

The bright white light flashed and engulfed the smaller light. The glowing orb of energy stopped for a moment, pulsing and then settling over the train tracks. It was close enough now that Raymond and the boys could see it reflect off the polished rails.

Then it began to move forward again. Toward them.

"Okay, boys..." Raymond said, shakily. "Maybe we should get going." The three backed off the tracks, not taking their eyes off the light. Robert ran straight to the truck. Raymond and Johnny ran after him. The three piled into the old pickup. Raymond started it and spun the wheels more than he planned as he pulled out of the dirt and gravel lot.

The road was fully dark now. Inside the truck, the soft light of the dash and green glow of the radio illuminated the faces of the boys, giggling and smiling at the fear and scare they had, now long past. They never noticed Raymond, driving quite deliberately at a faster than usual speed. This time, both hands squeezed the steering wheel tight. His eyes continually glanced into the rear view mirror, even though no cars followed them.

The next day, the boys regaled their parents and grandparents with the story of the light, and how brave they were to watch it until it got "right up next to us!"

"Robert ran away," johnny teased.

"Only 'cause Raymond said we had to leave," Robert defended himself.

Their parents listened to the stories, happy to have the two off doing something different while they took care of the baby. They didn't want their two older sons bored, and were happy with the small adventure. Their grandfather laughed at the story, enjoying it and knowing more about it than he would tell. He didn't want to give away any secrets. Their grandmother encouraged them to go look for more ghosts in the woods behind the house, or the old abandoned house down the street.

Raymond didn't come by that day. He spent the day at work, with his mind distracted by the night before. Time seemed to go on slower than usual. Five o'clock felt like it would never come.

Finally, when the work day was over, instead of going home, he drove back up the road, toward Ahoskie. He stopped at the same place he had visited the evening before.

Once inside, he asked the woman behind the counter, "Hey, Henry been in today?"

"It's the strangest thing," she said, with a puzzled look on her face, "He was supposed to come in this afternoon. I been here all day waiting for him. But no one's seen him since he left last night."

North Carolina Takes Care Of Its Own

March 17, 1865
Near Bentonville

"I should have stayed retired," General Joseph Johnston cursed at the very ground upon which he stood. The dark, rich ground that normally grew fertile crops and tall shade trees had turned into a murky clinging grime as the remnants of his army had marched a begrudging tactical manoeuvre through the coastal plains of North Carolina. "Army," he thought. "I can hardly call it an army."

The soldiers had been put together from various bits and pieces of other units that had fallen apart as the Confederacy collapsed under the weight of Grant and Sherman's attacks. Johnston had soldiers from as far as Tennessee and his home in Virginia. The Tennessee soldiers were more a hindrance than a help. They had no weapons, no ammo, no shoes, and no pay. The North Carolinian soldiers were of little help, as they had no desire to fight alongside troops from other states.

Johnston didn't care about the squabbles in the ranks. He just needed to find a way to somehow slow down Sherman's inevitable march of destruction through the Carolinas and into Virginia. He needed to secure good ground for a battle, as well as attack Sherman at a weak point. He needed a victory that wouldn't cost too many lives on his side. He also needed to make sure that Sherman didn't find him before he was ready.

That was the order that currently filtered down among the officers through the ranks. It ultimately fell upon Captain Aaron Wade, who commanded a small group of North Carolina soldiers, with a larger number of Tennessee and Virginia men attached. "At this time, we need to assure that Sherman won't be coming up from here," he pointed at a main road coming up from the south, "and overlapping from the north above us, here."

"What about this area?" asked another officer.

"That's all marsh and swamp. It is way too slow. No one would come up through there," commented a Tennessee major.

"I dunno," Wade responded. "Get Dalton in here. He's from this area. He would know if it is passable."

James Dalton, nothing but a private for the Confederates, and only wanting to be a civilian again, was hustled into the meeting full of officers that he desperately tried to avoid. "Dalton, you are from here. Do you think that an army could move through this area? It looks like it is full of pocosins and swamp. Could you move soldiers through there?"

"Aw, h-, uh, yessir," Dalton stammered. He hated officers. "You gotta realize, uh, sir, that might be all wet, but there are tons of raised mounds and dry land hidden in those woods. You could easy get men through there. It'd take time, but there are plenty of places to hide."

The major was not impressed. "They would not be foolish to march up through a swamp."

"Beggin' the major's pardon," implored Dalton, "but Sherman's been a marchin' all the way up from Georgia with no problem. He ain't gonna be slowed by no swamp."

"Major," responded Captain Wade, hoping to distract Dalton's insolence, "we need to consider this. If they get a force of any size there, they can hit our unprotected flank."

"Well," the major still wasn't happy about Dalton's disrespect, "send this man and some pickets, with an officer! To spy for any intrusions to our flank from this... swamp." He said it with both a tone of derision and pleasurable torment.

So, two hours later, Dalton was wandering through a mix of mossy peat bogs and forested canopy filled with pines and twisted hardwoods. A walk through the woods wasn't punishment for him. "The way this war is going," Dalton thought, "I could just keep walkin' and they'd never even miss me." The only problem was that he would have to separate himself from the other soldiers with him first. Especially the officer.

"I heard you coming, sir," Dalton whispered as Lieutenant Braighton marched his way up to where Dalton hid behind a scrubby tangle of bushes. The lieutenant was a younger recruit from Virginia, and it seemed to Dalton that he stepped on every branch on the ground the man could find.

Braighton for a moment was quiet, humbled by the insult, but then regained his posture. He was the officer here. "There is nothing but squirrels here, and darned little of those," he responded. "The Union Army is nowhere near here."

"You do not know that, sir, and Sherman's men are coming up from Fayetteville as we sit here. They just turned that entire city to dust and stone." Reports were already trickling in of the utter destruction of Fayetteville's weapons factory. Sherman had it blown to bits and then set fire to the remains for good measure. "There could be a thousand men right out there, and you could not see them." Dalton pointed out into the wilderness of the pocosins.

Dalton picked up his satchel and rifle. He began his march forward without waiting for a dismissal from the lieutenant. "What was he going to do, shoot me? He would get lost trying to get back," Dalton thought.

They walked slowly across the deep pine forest. The sun sank lower in the sky through the last days of winter. Beams of light filtered through the leaves and needles, turning the sky soft and orange, imbuing the forest with a delicate patina of ochre. A chill settled in.

This time, Dalton didn't hear Lieutenant Braighton until he got close. "We need to find a place to bivouac, Private. It is getting late and we need to prepare for the night."

Dalton agreed. No one should or would be moving through the pocosins at night, at least. There were too many dangers. It would be cold, slow going. And Dalton didn't want to have to drag any of these Tennessee recruits, or the Virginia officer, through this muck in the dark.

"We will camp on that low meadow there," Dalton pointed out a shaded and hidden patch of green moss that was separated from a shallow Carolina Bay by a thick copse of trees.

"Why not there?" Braighton pointed at a more open area on the far bank of the bay.

"Because, sir," Dalton did his best to keep the derision out of his voice, "it is in the open, we would be easily discovered, and it is not defensible. No fires, either, sir. The enemy would see the smoke. They may see the flame at this close a range."

"No fire?" Braighton was not happy about that. "It is going to be a cold night. And the men are not going to be happy about not having hot food."

They could eat their beans cold, Dalton thought. They had no meat to cook in the first place. "Better cold and hungry than dead or a prisoner," he said, just loud enough that the other soldiers could hear.

The dark came on quickly, and so did the cold. As much as Dalton was unhappy with being around the Tennessee boys, or the Virginia officer, they all huddled close under their blankets to keep off the cool evening. The sun had set to a burning red far to the west. In the sky, above the tree tops several thin wisps of smoke appeared. They twisted into nothingness, but gave away the fires of men, not close, but not so far away, either. "See that, Lieutenant? That is why we are here. And that is why we do not have a fire."

Lieutenant Braighton was quiet. He realized the private was right. Several fires burned in the west, meaning there were groups of men gathering. The group got quieter. They realized the danger and importance of their task.

"Dalton," Braighton asked quietly, "what is it you do not like about us? We are all here together, we serve, and fight, and..." he paused, not wanting to say that they die together. "What is it about us?"

Dalton was uncomfortable discussing this, especially with an officer. But he never was one to hold his tongue. It got him in trouble, but it was worth it. Usually.

"Look at those Volunteer boys," he took in all the Tennessee conscripts that huddled nearby. "You think they want to be here? They want to be home. Maybe fighting for Tennessee, maybe just home with their mommas. They do not want to be here. They don't have shoes or uniforms or pay even. If you gave them a moment, I bet they would walk right out of here and keep going until they found the mountains.

"It is not that I don't like you, or them. I think we would be better off without you. We would be better without Sherman turning our towns to powder. North Carolina doe not need all these people in it. We do not need all these soldiers here to win or lose a war we did not want. North Carolina takes care of its own."

"But there are so few of us left. Johnston needed an army."

"That's because all the North Carolinians are with Lee fighting a war in Virginia," Dalton pointed out. "Or already dead."

It was a sobering thought to the lieutenant. He didn't have any answer to sending off conscripts to fight and die. People fought best for their own land. "What did you do, before the war, Private?"

"I was a fisherman," Dalton waved his arm dismissively toward the east. "I had a boat out in the sound."

"Are you going back to that? After the war is over?"

"Naw," said Dalton. "I cannot. My boat got blown up."

Braighton was aghast. "How did that happen?"

Dalton shrugged, "Someone shot it with a cannon." How else, during this time, he thought.

The discussion wasn't going the way anyone liked. Lieutenant Braighton ordered the men to rest for the night. It was going to be a difficult sleep, with them on the ground with no covers other than the blankets they brought. But soldiers were soldiers, and they found a way to sleep anywhere. Dalton told them to stay away from the trees. Bugs would crawl on them in the night.

The night brought a fitful sleep. The men tossed, trying to find a comfortable place in the mossy earth. Dreams of dark monsters in Union uniforms crawled through the minds of some soldiers. Others dreamed of their mother and home. When they awoke, if any man knew of what the other dreamed, they would debate as to which was more traumatic. Instead they arose quietly, and only compared aches. "We should get moving," was all Dalton said. The sun was already rising, which meant they were visible.

It took an hour to cross around the first shallow bay and the nearby spongy march. They approached a large open field, green with new growth. "There are open raised lands like this all through this area," Dalton explained. They could hold a thousand men hidden in the marshes. He insisted they stay deep within the woods, instead of crossing over the open grassy mound. "We cannot leave footprints in that soft marsh."

There were several turtle back hills within the pocosins and forest. Many were big enough to hold hundreds of soldiers. Most had tall hardwood trees growing freely in the rich wet soil. They grew wide. There was no need to reach up yet, so they reached out with their branches instead, to gather the sunlight with a low wide canopy.

Dalton kept moving ahead. He walked carefully and silently. He always sought out cover to hide before moving forward. The rest of the men followed him. He was fine with that. At least they wouldn't give themselves away. He stopped at a particularly thick tangle of knotted up trees all covered in moss and lichens. A trail of ants, large and black, all dull exoskeletons in uncaring efficiency marched up and down the tree. They made no notice of Dalton as they climbed the chiseled bark.

Dalton felt something at his back, close. He realized it was Lieutenant Braighton's breathing. "What is it, Dalton?" he asked.

"I heard something." It was a simple statement. It took a moment to notice there was no noise. The birds were not singing now. No squirrels scurried and chattered in the trees. Far off, something splashed in shallow water. "Tell the men to take cover."

Braighton signaled the Tennessee boys to find any place to hide. Even he could hear the sounds now. It was more than one thing. There was a thump, a splash, and the soft clanging jangle that only came from the sounds of men with military gear.

Out of the woods in front of them burst a soldier in blue. His uniform was crisp and colorful, but disheveled. He looked like he had got up half dressed. He was coming straight toward Dalton and the rest of the men. And he wasn't trying to hide, at all. He made enough noise that anyone would know he was coming from hundreds of feet away.

Dalton, tucked in the nook of a tree trunk, pulled a long knife from a sheath strapped to his back. Braighton eyed it quietly with wonder. The blade was clearly a foot long, sharpened to a point, like a long thin triangle. It was an efficient weapon for making a deep stab wound while remaining silent. If the soldier saw them, and got away...

But there was nothing to worry about. The young soldier ran by them without noticing or reacting. He was moving fast. He scarcely noticed the branches slapping at him, but he did scream once when tripped by a large root. No one fired or attacked the soldier. He seemed more of a panicked kid than a threat. Dalton heard him whimper and cry as he ran.

Dalton and Braighton looked at each other. They were stunned and unsure as to what was happening. The lieutenant almost stood up to look when six more soldiers ran by with the same terrified look. They disappeared into the forest. A mix of cries and screams permeated the morning.

It took a full minute for Dalton to move again. When everything was again silent, he rose slowly from his hiding place and paced forward deliberately.

They had only been a grove of trees away from the small Union encampment, it turned out. It was less than a half a mile away from them. On another of the tree lined mossy hillocks, the small Union force had set up their camp for the night. The remnants of campfires still smoldered in the late morning.

"How come they have not left?" wondered Dalton in his head.

He stopped for only a moment to look over the encampment. There were backpacks, a few tents, some blankets, and many rifles. But Dalton could see no soldiers. Not a one. No one drinking coffee or eating. There were all the signs of life, but no life anywhere. "Except for the trees,"

Dalton thought. He stood from his hiding spot and began walking into the camp.

Braighton tried to call out to him, but worried about alerting the Union camp. It looked big enough to hold five hundred men. It would have been a dangerous threat to their unprotected flank if it had made it undiscovered through the pocosins. They could have hit Johnston's flank, done damage, and disappeared back into the swamps before anyone could have reacted. Then he realized. They already disappeared.

Dalton walked unmolested into the camp. Nothing happened. Nothing at all. Braighton gave in to his curiosity and marched in behind Dalton. The Tennessee boys wandered to the edge, curious but timid. A group of ten would stand no chance against an army this size.

"Where are the men?" Braighton asked.

Dalton looked around. There was absolutely no one in any part of the camp. He walked around the trees, old wide oaks and other hardwoods that grew thick and short in the open mossy field. Roots reached out into the soft soil to drink from the tannic water that filled the low spots throughout the region. The trees looked strange to Dalton. Familiar.

He tripped over a root and stumbled, but caught himself. He looked down, then gasped. Dalton jumped back, his hand going to his shoulder to draw his long bladed knife. Then he stopped himself.

Braighton joined him and looked at what Dalton had seen. It wasn't a root that tripped him. It was a leg. A Union soldier stuck his foot out to trip Dalton. He could tell it was a

Union soldier by the new boot he wore, and the blue wool pants leg. That was all he could see.

The rest of the soldier was entombed in the trunk of the tree.

The soldier's body was wrapped with the bark and wood of the tree. Under the wooden crust, it was easy to see the distinct outline of a soldier. His details had been roughed over, but Dalton could see the man's buttons on his coat, raised up ever slightly in the bark. His face was lifted up and back, his mouth open slightly, as if frozen in an intake of breath.

Dalton then realized why the trees looked so strange, and so familiar. He looked out at the copse of trees, hundreds of them, all growing around the raised hill. All of them had strange lumps at the bottom of them.

"Dear God," one of the Tennessee boys half cursed, half prayed, in a soft sigh.

"What happened to them?" Lieutenant Braighton asked, aghast and terrified.

Dalton reached down at the foot of the soldier that had tripped him. All the other soldiers around him had been completely entombed. Their legs were stretched out from the trees. The roots had grown up around them, hiding the legs and feet. They looked just like the thick roots that reached deep into the soil. Dalton touched the exposed leg. It shook and trembled slightly. The leg was still warm.

He stood up, but said nothing. Dalton suddenly felt like he needed to wipe his hand on something for a very long time.

"What happened, Private?" Braighton asked again.

"Look, all around," Dalton took in the horrid scene throughout the copse of trees. "They did just what any soldier would. They leaned up against these trees. They probably rested there after eating. Soldiers can sleep anywhere." Dalton looked down at the poor soldier encased in the tree at his feet. A big black ant crawled across the soldier's face. "They just fell asleep under the trees. Then the trees just took'em. All of them, except those poor kids we saw running away. All the rest got taken in by these big ol' Carolina oaks and sweetgums."

The entire field was covered in a wooden graveyard. The Union soldiers were imprisoned in tombs made of the tree trunks, all captured, imprisoned, and buried.

"They should not have come through here," Dalton said with finality.

"I told you, Lieutenant. North Carolina takes care of its own."

The Lake Cammack Creature

Lake Cammack
1932

North Carolina has its share of natural wonders. From the mountains to the ocean, our outdoors are still an organic and evergrowing part of the state. The Longleaf Pine flourishes wherever it drops its seeds. Throughout the state are the mysterious Carolina Bays, shallow ponds that dot the landscape, without leaving a hint as from where they came. Even the many man-made lakes hold strange mysteries.

There are several lakes formed by dams in the state. Impounded long ago to provide water for the ever growing population, or just for recreation, these lakes seem innocuous on the surface. But underneath they hold their secrets in cold, still water. Lake Lure has a town under it, complete with a preserved church. Farther west, Fontana Lake not only inundated a town, but the roads to it as well, when the dam was built to provide power to western North Carolina.

Then there is Lake Cammack. Smaller than other lakes, it sits, relatively unknown outside of the locals who recreate on the water there, kayaking or fishing. But it holds a secret along its reedy banks.

When the lake was impounded back in 1932, there was no town to move or residents to relocate. It was mostly a natural shallow plain filled with brush and a few patches of red earth farmland. There was one, only one, small house on the land. A reclusive man, not entirely a hermit, but certainly not friendly, lived a quiet life by the river, hunting, fishing, and growing a small plot of vegetables to get him through each year. When the county reached out to him, he had little to say back, and none of it good, when he was told he would have to give up his home and leave the flood plain. When the Alamance County government became more insistent, he became more contrary.

Soon when public servants, men with papers to be served and plans to be enacted, showed up, they were greeted with the wide business end of a hunting shotgun. The old man's property line became as far as someone dared to step into the range of the weapon's buckshot. When the planners became desperate, they then found not only the weapon, but locked doors and boarded up windows. A large plain sign with large plain letters went up at the property's edge. Keep Out.

Ultimately, the engineers and councils and deputies all agreed that they would just leave the old man where he was. When the water started coming up, he'd come out on his own. It would take over a year to fill the lake. He would have plenty of time to change his mind.

But the old man didn't change his mind. It took a month for the river to overflow to the old house. Still the old man never appeared. The door and windows stayed boarded and closed. When the water got up past the top of the windows, something odd happened. The lake stopped filling.

Engineers were at their wits end. The level should continue up, slowly of course, they agreed, but it should still be changing. The river still flowed, but the water never crested the ceiling of the house. It would not go higher. The engineers checked the dam. There was no problem with it. No water escaped at the far end. There were no other places for the water to flow. It had to be somewhere. Ultimately, they decided that there must be a small aquifer somewhere that was filling, and once that filled, the water would go up again.

And then, after about a month, the water rose. It took another year, but the fields flooded, and Lake Cammack was born. The men who tried to force the old man out of his home conveniently forgot about him. They defended their actions by saying he had plenty of time to get out. But the house stayed boarded up, all the time the lake flooded. The door and window never opened.

It was a little over a year later, and the lake was full. Life found the waters nearby, and reeds grew in the shallows.

Birds sang in the cattails, while ducks flew in to the water. Deer strolled the grassy banks. Late at night, raccoons and opossums wandered the wetlands, hunting for plentiful food. The engineers and county agents and council members all showed up as the water began to lap at the sides of the dam. The lake was done. It was full. No one even asked what happened to the old man in the house, now submerged deep below the lake.

The councilman who tried so hard to run the old man out stood at the edge of the lake. The area had already been cleared for an automobile lot, a fishing pier, and a boat ramp. This would be the center of life getting on the lake, he thought. He was proud of his effort to push the lake impound through. He helped raise money, hire workers, and get the dam built. This was his lake, no matter what anyone else said publicly.

Just north of the newly cleared land was a shallow bay, filled with new green reeds that were beginning to glow with the color of sunset. He squinted, thinking he was seeing things in the reeds. Hidden within the tall grass, he spied two glowing eyes, red and burning, looking at him. The councilman rubbed his eyes, not sure at what he saw. Was there a person over there, hiding in the lake? Hiding in *his* lake?

He wandered over to look in the shallows as the sky darkened into twilight.

He was never seen again.

A few months later, the engineer that planned the lake had been inspecting the dam. Alone on one side, he noticed in the new growth that benefited from the high water that something looked out from the plants and trees. Something with red eyes. When others at the dam heard a scream, cut off in the middle, they found the man missing. But atop the dam were wet footprints that led off into the lake.

Over the next year, several people who were responsible for building the lake or running the old man off his property had gone missing or mentioned seeing strange red eyes along the lake shore.

Over the years, the various sportspeople that enjoyed the lake have reported seeing the red eyes glaring through the reeds and grasses. A shape of a man, not much of a man, all dark, slimy, looking more like a giant salamander than a human, had been seen late in the evening, moving through the rushes. Boaters keep a wide berth from any water where they see those glowing red eyes.

When the story is told of the old man, the house and the lake, or the missing people, most locals wave it off as not even legend. It's just a strange story. But there are those who have been at Lake Cammack that still wonder what happened deep in its waters long ago.

One person, a later employee who helped manage the lake, is one of those people. A new marina was discussed to be built just north of the parking lot. It would have meant cutting down the reeds and grasses along the little bay. He argued it was unnecessary. It also would ruin a perfectly nice natural area. His convincing argument kept the development from going through.

The day after he had won the debate, he wandered out to the parking lot and looked over at the reeds. He wasn't sure what he saw, but it looked like red eyes glaring out from the tall cattails. He walked over, through the trees, along the shore, and to the line of cattails. There, pounded and stabbed into the muddy ground, was an old and decrepit sign. He scraped away layers of film to see it clearly. It read, simply...

Keep Out

The Cries of Little Louise

Davidson College
1893

In the early days of medical study, the routines and ethics of the students, professors, and doctors of medical schools were not as principled as they would become in later years. One of the expectations of a medical student was that they had to acquire their own cadaver in order to perform autopsies for forensic study of the body and its functions.

While at the time death was a common event, as few people died of old age in an era of disease, infection, and injury, getting the bodies was less simple. When a person passed, the family understandably wanted to pay their last respects and allow the body, and the soul, to rest in peace. They were noticeably reticent in providing the remains to students who would be clinically intimate, yet emotionally distant with a family member who was loved and lost.

This lead to the rise of the gruesome and ghoulish job of the grave robber. Their emotions steeled and stilled to heartlessness, they would be constantly on the lookout for the newly dead. If a person passed away, they would plot to find the grave, often on the same night as the burial, in order to disinter the corpse before it began to decompose.

So it was, on a night in 1893, that two medical students from the newly formed medical school at Davidson College asked for help in acquiring the body of a girl who died unexpectedly in nearby Salisbury. Their henchman, Old Thomas, insisted upon the two students to come along. He had no quibbles about hauling a dead body out of a grave, but he insisted they help dig the dirt. Old Thomas wasn't old, but he was quite terrifying looking. Tall, thin, and sallow, with his pale pallor a consequence of working more nights than days, he was a presence to behold. Most students preferred to behold him as little as possible.

So the students decided to ride their own horses while Thomas drove the wagon on their way to Salisbury.

It was well after midnight when the three arrived at the little graveyard. There was only a sliver of a moon that cast just enough light to show vague shadows of grave markers made out of wood that delineated the final resting places of the families buried there. When one of the students asked about a lantern, Old Thomas hushed him, "No lights. People are gonna be watchin'."

They found the grave as much by feel as by sight. A fresh wooden slat marked the soft earth that had been turned over and out to dig the poor girl's grave. It was too dark to read the name, Louise Coble, and no one there cared who she was anyway. They hurried, working as fast as they could without making noise. Wisps of clouds sliced the moon, obscuring their vision. The two students didn't mind the darkness. For all their clinical dispositions, the pale white face of Thomas looking down on them as they re-dug a grave was a chilling sight. They put their back into their work with haste, and were rewarded with a soft *thunk* for their efforts. The family had rushed the burial, and had placed the coffin, a simple wooden box, only three feet down.

"Git out," commanded Thomas softly, but with a firm bite of hate toward the two students. There was dirty work to do, and he was the one to do it.

They climbed out, perhaps not happily, but at least with relief of not having to do the last bit of work that Old Thomas was paid so well to do. They saw him leap down into the shallow grave, where there was a soft rending of cheap wood, and then the sound of the heavy cotton tarp being unfolded. A lump wrapped in the cloth came up over Thomas' shoulder, without definition, but completely obvious as to the nature of the object. The corpse was smaller than the students had expected.

They left the graveyard quietly. They didn't bother to fill in the grave.

The ride back to Davidson was silent for many reasons. Thomas didn't want to talk. The students had other conversations in their head. And poor Louise had recently lost any ability to complain about her lot.

It was in the dead of the morning, after four o'clock, when the wagon and riders arrived back at the college. The three pulled up to the rear of Chambers Hall, where the body would be stored before the autopsy later that same day. The students had dismounted and stood near the back of the wagon, waiting for Thomas to do his last deed and carry the body into the cooler rooms for storage. Thomas stood idle at the back.

"I want my pay."

A stoic and steadfast man with the corpse of a girl on his wagon was no one with whom to dicker. A price was agreed and a price was paid. Thomas carried the body inside and left into the remaining night. The students went back to their dormitory for a few hours rest. Sleep came to them. They felt fortunate that exhaustion had done its best job at hiding away dreams or nightmares into the deepest recesses of their minds.

The next evening, a few groups of students gathered around their procured cadavers. No one said a thing as to how they were acquired. Rarely was a body donated, though it did happen. The students, as well as the professors, all pretended that each cadaver was the one exception. It was a necessary step, the doctors would say. "Ibi Mortui Vivos Docent." Let the dead teach the living.

The other cadavers were old, with the injuries that went into a rough life. Scars on the face or a fresh wound often told a simple and obvious story of their death. Others were worn and damaged by time. No one else had a young girl.

The class was commenced, time and lesson passed, and class was ended. The bodies would be, mostly, removed and interred in a potter's field. The graves were scattered and unmarked. No one even knew the names of the dead, much less where they would rest. They merely were placed in a certain portion of the field, while other sections lay fallow. There was no desire to turn over a not too fresh grave.

The students returned to their studies and tried to put all thoughts of the past few days out of their heads, which was not an easy task.

But then, after a few days, sounds were heard in Chambers Hall.

The plaintive cry of a girl was heard in otherwise empty hallways. When people went to investigate, no person was found. After a few days, the cries turned into shrieks. Then into wails of anguish. At night, the screams became a regular occurrence. It drove many of the staff out of the building. Some swore not to return, day or night, until the source was found. They believed a girl was loose, hiding somewhere in the building. The local police were called to investigate, but no one could find any girl hiding in the building. Even watching the doors to see if someone snuck in didn't help. The doors remained closed and locked, yet the whimpering cries continued.

Soon, doors opened and closed on their own. Items were found moved, or knocked off the desks and shelves. It was of particular notice that the tables and trays used for autopsies had shifted noticeably in the night, even as Chambers Hall was dark and empty. Students began to wonder just who would be willing to wander the shadowy halls where the autopsies were performed, because no person would have the courage to do that. No one in their dormitories was willing to go near the hall, much less in it, late at night.

Then they began to speculate. Maybe no one living was willing to do so.

Maybe it was a ghost. A girl.

Only one girl had been brought in for an autopsy.

The students had avoided the local newspapers out of concern of seeing their deed written in ink. But now everyone looked. They learned the name, Louise Coble, and how her family was distraught. Then they all realized that poor Louise wanted to go home. She cried every night, alone, afraid, and unsure as to what had happened to her in her last, final sleep.

The police were again called, but this time more surreptitiously. Quiet and grave requests were made by the deans, professors, and even the wealthy donors, to help right something while not recognizing how wrong it was.

The students and staff attempted to gather the remains of Louise, digging what they could from the soft earth of the potter's field. Her earthly remains were then returned, without ceremony but with a hefty dose of judgement by the poor family that had lost her, not once, but twice.

The students thought they had solved the problem. Now that Louise was back in her grave, the cries would stop.

A week later, the whimpers and sobs were heard again. This time, softer, more forlorn.

They became more faint over time, but they never stopped. Chambers Hall became known to be haunted. Most staff adjusted their times to not be there late at night, or alone. But the cries carried on. The doors still opened and closed, and items were rearranged. To say the staff and students got used to it would be an exaggeration. They used it as a warning.

Curiously, the ghostly sounds did finally vanish. In 1921, the ghostly crying of Louise disappeared once and for all. Chambers Hall burned to ashes that year. It would not be replaced until the end of the decade. The remains of the first building can still be seen in the yard of the new hall, where all the grass over the line that was the original foundation dies every summer.

Joe Sledge

The Lights Of Fear

Buxton
1982

Henry Gaskins swore an oath worthy of a twelve year old as his fingers slipped while tying a knot on his fishing lure. "Dangit!" he blasphemed softly, and under his breath. He was hurrying, wanting to get fishing before it got too hot and the fish went away. As he was finishing up his knot, he saw the twisted twine of his crab line jerk and move. He had a blue on the line. He dropped his pole and grabbed his net, quickly scooped up the big blue crab and threw it in a bucket with the others. The old fish head went back in the water with a splash. His family was having a reunion party tonight. They would eat well, if he had something to do with it.

Henry sat on his neighbor's pier, jutting out into the shallows of the Pamlico Sound, as he fished and caught blue crabs. Across the water, only fifty feet or so, was his grandfather's pier. It was older, thicker, with the patina of age and weather from seeing storms and hurricanes. He liked his grandfather's dock better. But the fishing was never good there.

Finally tying a line, he made his first cast. He liked using lures. They were harder work. Fish would jump at worms or shrimp. Catching on a lure was a challenge. It made the fish taste better.

As the sun spun through the sky, it got hotter on the dock. Henry stood up and walked toward the soft silty shore. The soundside was a different texture than the beach. The sand was packed firm, and had a waxy feel. It made walking much easier. The shade of the trees helped, too. The deer flies weren't much fun, though, Henry said to himself as he swatted with his sweaty cap. "Just a few more casts," he thought. "Maybe I'll get lucky and catch something in Grampa's back yard."

But each time, the lure came back empty. Henry cast once more, and just let the lure flop into the water. He put his cap back on, wiped sweat from his brow, and then reeled the hook in. He felt a strange tug on the line, but when he pulled, there was weight on the other end. The line didn't give. He knew he had hit a snag. Henry pulled again, and felt something give slightly on the other end, and the lure came free. He reeled it up through the muck.

The lure flopped around as Henry tried to grab it and hook it to an eye of his rod. That was when he noticed something on the hook. It was a tarnished and corroded piece of metal, roughly in the shape of a plus sign. It was strange looking, so Henry kept it.

The rest of the day went well. They steamed the crabs for lunch. A long line of newspaper covered the backyard picnic table, along with a long line of paper towels. The crabs, now red and not blue, were picked and cracked, covered with liberal doses of Old Bay seasoning or hot sauce or vinegar and black pepper or whatever any of the family thought was appropriate. Bits of corn and potatoes filled out the meal. Everyone kept forgetting which cup was theirs. Henry's mother said, "As long as we keep the germs in the family!"

The evening was more sedate, as the women went to the kitchen, the men to the front porch, the teenagers, Henry's cousins mostly, ran to the darkness of the woods, and the little ones played around the house. The only other person close to Henry's age was his ten year old cousin Ashley, who had her nose happily pressed in a book while she sat by the window. With no one to play with, Ashley's idea seemed like as good an idea as any, Henry said, and went upstairs to read a book in his room as he looked out over the glistening Pamlico Sound. The moon was up and full. The water had only the slightest breeze moving it, which made the moonlight reflect diamonds into the inky water. Henry held an old book of Outer Banks legends in his hand. It smelled of musty paper and salt and everything that was anything in the old house. He didn't open it, but instead stared out at the sound, waiting to see the light of a boat go by.

Instead, he saw something else. The small secluded cove that was the back of his family's ancestral home was framed by the long new dock of his neighbors on the right, and a grassy peninsula lined with trees to the left. Grampa's old dock was somewhere in the middle. Henry noticed the water didn't glisten there. It was all glorious black, like the night, but starless. Onyx smooth, the water could appear bottomless in the night. He knew it was only a few feet deep, but it was fun to imagine. Only Henry's imagination was not engaged now. He saw within the waters a strange glow. Unlike the white crystalline gleam of the moonlight, there was a green radiance, and it came from under the water, not reflected on it. The light reminded him of the strange fish, the mysterious hunters he saw in books, that lived in the darkened depths and made their own luminescence.

But this was no deep sea diving excursion. Henry watched the light form. Then more appeared. He counted once he saw more than five. "Eight, nine... ten," he said in his head. The lights seemed to roll with the waves. They were long, about five or six feet. The lights moved back and forth, always getting close to the shore, but never making it.

After watching for a few moments, Henry got up and ran for the door. He wanted to see what they were up close.

Out the door, out the back, he ran down the walkway that was lined with large twisted Live Oaks, branches meant for climbing that reached out in the darkness to snatch away a kid to keep for themselves. Henry had no time for imaginary games to relish, no pirates in the wind. He wanted to get to the sound and see the lights.

But when he got there, the lights were gone.

He walked back up the long wooden walkway, back to the house. Deep from the trees on either side came a plaintive moan, the call of a ghost out for a good scare. Henry just kept walking. He had no interest in ghost games now, his disappointment was that strong. He wondered if his cousins, older boys, had been playing a joke on him.

"Hey Henry!" a figure jumped out of a tree near him, "c'mon, we're gonna go check out the old house down the road!" Henry recognized one of his cousins, a fifteen year old named Rodney that always seemed to be plotting some kind of torment. Henry kept walking until he was far enough away, then, at a trot, said, "Get bent!" If they were fooling with him by making those lights, he wasn't going to give them the satisfaction. He ran toward the back of the house. His cousin attempted to give chase, but gave up quickly when he hit the soft yellow lights of the back porch and the view of his mother.

Henry went in and watched TV until bedtime.

The next day, most of the family was out exploring or on the beach. He sat, alone, and happy, on the back dock. His fishing pole hung in his hands, the line lifeless even as a bobber held up a fresh worm.

His mind otherwise occupied, Henry didn't notice the dock moving for a moment or two. Footsteps softly shook the pier. It didn't matter, thought Henry, there's no fish to scare away. Henry looked up to see his grampa walking down the old wood dock to him.

"Hey, Hank!" Grampa Michael Midgett always called Henry 'Hank', which Henry really liked. "Got any boites?" Henry's grampa was an old Banker, a Hoi Toider who spoke with the soft accents of Hatteras Island and the Outer Banks, where they make "oi" instead of the hard "I". Every soft sound, the normally deep vowels that ended words, droned out in a sweet nasal brogue.

Henry looked up and squinted into the risen sun, and shook his head. "Nope. Not a nibble." He was quiet for a moment, not sure what to say, then he asked, "Hey, Grampa, you ever have luck fishing out here? I never catch anything here."

"No, Oi don't fish out here often, though," he responded. Michael Midgett, even though he was only 65, was the elder statesman of the clan, and the most experienced sportsman in a family of outdoor loving people. He stood quietly next to Henry while a thought played across his mind. Henry couldn't see the gears turning in his grampa's head. The sun was too bright, and Henry had thoughts of his own. He stood up.

"I never catch anything here," he complained. "Over there," he pointed to the neighbor's dock, "No problem, I catch crabs and fish all the time. Out on the point," he gestured at the spit of land covered with trees and grass behind him, "Lots of fish. But here, and on the shore, nothing.

"The only thing I ever hooked was this," he said and took the strange metal item he hooked the day before out of his pocket. "You know what this is?"

"You got this yesterday?" Michael asked.

"Yeah," answered Henry. "And, the funniest thing," he almost wasn't sure to add what happened last night. "When everyone else was out after dinner, I saw the strangest thing out here last night. I saw a bunch of lights in the water."

"What koind of loights?" Michael asked. He hoped the boy was just seeing boats far out on the sound.

"Weird green lights, right there," he pointed into the shallow bay next to the dock. "Like, I dunno, big glowing jellyfish in the water, I guess."

"Loights? More than one?" Henry noticed the first thing his grampa asked was how many lights, not a statement that he didn't believe Henry.

"Yeah."

"Haow many?"

"Maybe ten."

Michael suddenly felt the air go hot, then cold. This was what he had been thinking about. "You know your my favorite grandson, roight?"

And Henry did know that. His family, his siblings and cousins all liked Grampa, but Henry was the only one with a nickname. He worked the boat with his grandfather, spent evenings and mornings fishing or working together while the others played or swam. Clearly the genes had passed more deeply to this grandchild than others. "Yeah," he said quietly, and respectfully, "I know. And you're my favorite grampa!" Henry smiled at the little joke.

"C'mon insoide, Oi gotta tell ya somethin'."

Inside, away from the early summer sun and the insects it brought, the air conditioning purred cool air throughout the house. It was just the two of them, and Michael was perfectly happy with that. He poured some lemonade. Drinks were in order.

"Now, Oi gotta tell you something, something that even your mother doesn't know. Most people around here don't know abaout this, and those of us that do don't talk abaout it. But maybe you need to know. Someone's gotta know to keep the story. Not tell, you gotta promise. No telling. Anyone. Oi know it's not good to keep secrets from yer mama, but this one, well, you'll see when Oi tell you. But you gotta promise, 'kay?"

Henry was intrigued. His grampa never led him down any secret or dark place before. He knew he could trust the man. "Promise," he said.

"Okay, so sit and listen, boy...

"Now, you know, Oi was in the war," Michael nodded to the frame on the wall that had only a few souvenirs of his time in World War II. Some campaign ribbons and a few medals, along with a large sheathed knife were all that were on display. Henry recognized the Purple Heart, but didn't know what the many others meant.

"But Oi was already old when Oi joined up. Oi was 26. Oi was working here on the oisland when war broke out, and served here for a whoile until Oi got sent to the Pacific. Now, back then, it was tough. We had nothing, and couldn't get much more than nothing. That lemonade?" he lifted his glass, dripping with condensation, cold with ice, "we never came close to having that. Lemons were scarce, and sugar was near impossible, hoighly rationed. All we had was a bunch of Nazi submarines off the coast, sinking ships left and roight. We were always scared of going aout on the beach. You definitely couldn't go aout at noight. The boys on the shore patrols were all from inland, and they were jumpy as cats. They'd shoot at every little sound."

"What were they shooting at?" Henry asked.

"Oi'm getting to that," Michael eased into the story. "See, the big worry for us was spoies." Even the way he said spies made the term a little less scary. "We always worried that the Germans would put a boat aout from one of their U-boats loaded with explosives and spoies to blow up the coast guard station, or the Navy base, or even the loighthouse. We were scared, all of us. See, every noight, we'd hear a ship getting blowed up by a U-boat, loighting up the noight and burning up in the ocean. We'd see loifeboats all shot up with holes washed up on the beach, or even dead bodies. You seen that graveyard over by where the loighthouse is?"

Henry nodded his head.

"We had to bury a lot of bodies that washed up. But we were scared. It was dark toimes then, boy, dark toimes. We just weren't ready for that. We got scared, and a lot of us got suspicious.

"Whenever someone new showed up, people wondered who they were. Everyone was sure some couple, a man and a woman who got on the bus to go down to Ocracoke, were spoies. They stayed daown there, askin' questions abaout the Coast Guard and the Navy base. They went back north, we don't know what ever happened to them. Maybe they got caught, maybe they went back to Germany, no one knew.

"So whenever a stranger showed up, we got suspicious. When ten showed up, people got really suspicious.

"In late 1942, these ten boys showed up, lookin' for a place to stay. They said they were from Kinnakeet and Rodanthe. They all were workin' for the government, planning for ships to come in. But they needed a place to live and time to look around the island.

"They made a point of talking to the locals abaout sports, being from North Carolina, talkin' abaout stuff that was happening in the state, like they were showin' they were from here. Their English was great. They didn't sound loike no German spoies."

"But, see, boy, we don't sound loike no other American araound here, do we?" he said with a smile.

Henry shook his head, silent and focused. No one else talked like someone from Hatteras.

"They knew them boys weren't from Rodanthe, nor from Nags Head neither. Someone said it aout loud, and everyone started thinking it. They were Nazi spoies.

"Naow, no one knew what to do. They were afraid them boys would disappear, or blow something up, or kill a bunch of us like they had been doing for a year out on the Atlantic. But some of the folks here on the oisland just couldn't let them get away with anything. So when those fellers were aout, some oislanders broke in and went lookin' for clues. And you know what they foind?"

"What?" Henry asked excitedly. He imagined spy radios, rifles, pistols, explosives, Nazi banners and flags.

"Nothing. Not a thing there. Just some change a clothes, a few books, food, fishing poles, but no spoiy stuff.

"They were disappointed. These local fellers were sure they were spoies, but there was nothing that proved it. Then one day them strangers was walking round the dock and one of them got his shirt torn on a gaff, and in his pocket, he had one of these." Michael held up the tarnished metal item. "It's an iron cross. It's a medal for them Nazi boys to wear.

"See, if they were caught being spoies, they could get shot, but they figured if they had this hidden on them, well, that's enough of a uniform that they would just go to a prisoner of war camp instead. But they didn't figure on being caught by a couple of local fishermen."

"So, how did the iron cross end up in the water here?" asked Henry.

"Oi'm getting to that," insisted Michael. "Well, right then and there, the folks that caught them decided to take care of their own problems. See, them Nazis had been blowing up everything and filling the ocean with oil and bodies. So instead of capturing them and turning them over, the locals just did them in right there."

"They killed them?" Henry was surprised, but not shocked. Everyone knew what the Nazis had done, and how the U.S. had gone to war to stop them. They got what they deserved as far as he was concerned.

"Yeah, we were at war! So the Hatteras folks just did what everyone else was doing. They killed them all."

"Wait, so what does that have to do with fishing in the back yard?"

Michael thought for a moment, looking at the tarnished and pitted iron cross. "You say you saw lights out in the water last night? Well, let's see what happens tonight, you and me."

The rest of the day passed in aching anticipation. Finally, the twilight fell to darkness and Michael went to get his grandson. The two stood at the shore and waited. It took a long while, but then the light came. First one, then quickly more and more, up to ten lights, washing under the shallow water. Henry was in awe of the lights, but his grampa stood impassive and unimpressed. He looked at the water, then at Henry.

"See, boy, after the Nazis were killed, no one wanted to even bother burying them. They didn't belong on the same oisland as the rest of us. So, they just dumped the bodies in the sound.

"Right here." Michael pointed at the lights in the water.

"So, I know you caught it, but Oi don't think you want to keep this, do you?" he held out the iron cross to Henry, who took it and threw it without thought into the water.

"So," Henry asked, "are those things out there... ghosts?"

"You don't have to worry abaout those things," Michael answered. He took Henry's arm and led him to the water's edge. "They never get out of the water." With that statement, he stepped into the shallow water. The lights scattered and then disappeared. "They're afraid of me."

"Why?"

"Cause Oi'm the one that killed them."

Joe Sledge

Murder In The Randolph Mine

Gold Hill
1840

The discovery of gold in North Carolina came suddenly to the sprawling wilderness and rolling hills that climbed toward the west of the state. Little Gold Hill had its population grow as it dug the mines deep. Over five thousand souls moved in with the hopes of jobs and money. Gold Hill became so successful it was the envy of other towns in the area, including nearby Charlotte, where the mayor wished his town would be as prosperous as its neighbor.

With the miners came all the necessary and not so necessary establishments. Homes and boarding houses went up, along with saloons and brothels. The mines were exquisitely dangerous. Danger lurked at every darkened corner of the deep shafts and their long, narrow tracing veins. Disease ran rampant in the claustrophobic confines of the town. There was almost no medical care, and health concerns were non-existent for the miners. The mine owners had no concern with literally working the miners to death.

But if the mine didn't kill a man, and disease couldn't find purchase, there was always... murder.

Aaron Klein showed up in Gold Hill soon after the first mine shafts had been dug. He came from Pennsylvania with the same plans and ideals as any other person in Gold Hill. Get a job, get paid, and get rich. He got more than he bargained in more than one way.

Klein was not a common name in the area, but it was easily recognizable. He received dirty looks, hate filled glances, and the usual mumble that came from the hard edged anti-semitic bigots that crowded the mines and saloons. Most of them kept their comments to themselves, because Klein became well liked as a decent fellow, and a good worker. But one person made sure to let everyone, including Klein, know exactly how he felt.

Stan Kukla hated Klein. He hated everyone, but he really hated Aaron Klein. While being Jewish was Big Stan's main complaint, Kukla hated that Klein still was more well liked than he was, and that Klein was a good miner. But there was one other reason he hated Klein.

In a town filled with hard edged rough and tough miners, there was also a serious dearth of women. Aaron Klein not only had friends, but he also had a woman who fell in love with him.

Elizabeth Moyle was the most beautiful woman in the town. While most miners saw her as attractive, few ever even attempted to court her. They knew they were below her station. She was also the daughter of the manager of the Randolph Mine. They knew not to mess with the boss's daughter. And they gave Aaron Klein a bit more space as the future son-in-law.

But Stan Kukla couldn't stand that. There was no way that Klein deserved one of the few women in town, especially the beautiful Elizabeth. Kukla made it a daily occurrence to threaten and intimidate Klein. No one else would stand up to the big man and his threats. But no matter what he said, Kukla couldn't separate the two lovers. He had to move into more dastardly deeds.

One day, the little puppy that Aaron Klein owned, which followed its master to the mine every day and waited outside, was found dead, killed at the entrance to the Randolph Mine. Aaron Klein had disappeared. Everyone asked what had happened to Klein. Kukla explained that Aaron Klein had packed up and left unexpectedly that morning, heading back to Pennsylvania. While no one believed him, there was no Klein to be found. All of his things were still there. He had told no one that he was leaving. But he truly was gone.

People discussed, quietly, the thought that Kukla killed Klein, but there was no proof. And no body.

What did appear a few days later was a strange shimmering light at the entrance to the Randolph Mine. When it began to appear every day, other miners, sure that

Klein was dead, supposed it was the ghost of Aaron Klein. Each day it would be seen. Sometimes it appeared early in the morning. Other times it shone at the end of evening twilight. Most of the miners were sure it was the ghost of Klein, and were intrigued but not afraid.

Except for Kukla.

He was furious.

Stan Kukla was sure the ghost of Aaron Klein was coming back for him. He only got more frustrated and angry every time someone brought it up. He'd shout, thrash, and threaten anyone who said it, but the teasing and taunting didn't stop. And the light kept appearing.

Within a week, Stan Kukla could be seen, or heard, at the very bottom of the 850 foot shaft of the Randolph Mine, stumbling in the toxic darkness with only his weak lantern to guide him, bellowing an echoed curse with every shaky step that banged his body into the spoil rock that was cast into the pit. The rocks sat jagged and deadly at the very bottom. They pointed up as manmade stalagmites, a vicious bed of nails fit only for an evil giant. Which, everyone realized now, Stan Kukla was.

The miners now figured Kukla believed in the ghost tale, that Aaron Klein haunted the shaft, and haunted Stan Kukla for murdering him. Kukla was going mad, searching for the body he must have cast down the shaft to get rid of the evidence.

One morning the crew came to the entrance to the Randolph Mine to find the skip, the mining car used to haul people up and down the main shaft, was not at the top. The skip was always placed at the top of the mine at the end of the day to both seal the opening from people and things falling down, and to make a quicker entrance for the next day's workers.

The miners began running the skip up. It took a long time, too long to be at one of the branches along the shaft. It had been at the very bottom. When it finally came up to the morning daylight, Stan Kukla was on it, dead as can be.

There was plenty of speculation as to how Kukla died. He fell, being careless and worked up in the dark. His heart gave out, or he died of disease or lack of air in the shafts without anyone else there to monitor him. But quietly, everyone knew what really happened. Those that found him didn't like to say it, but Kukla's face was frozen, his eyes wide. A look of terror was in Kukla's still open eyes.

The ghost of Aaron Klein had come back and gotten revenge on Stan Kukla.

Everyone was sure of it, even if they didn't say it. All anyone did was point out that the light stopped appearing at the entrance to the Randolph Shaft.

In later years, visitors would tell of seeing a man out walking in the cloudy twilight on the trails around Gold Hill. He seems strange, pensive, both in thought and single minded in looking for someone. As they pass the man, they have the feeling to turn and see him once more, only to find he is gone.

Along the lake shore and near the old rock wall that lines the park and many shafts of old Gold Hill has been seen a spectral shape of a woman. After Aaron Klein's death,

Elizabeth Moyle never sought out another suitor. She never considered marriage. She died and was buried in the local graveyard.

While the vengeful spectre of Aaron Klein at the mine shaft long disappeared, it is thought that the two lovers still seek each other out, wandering the grounds they once knew in life, still attempting to reunite in the afterlife.

Mad Mag

Ocracoke
September, 1987

Adam Howard loved to scare the little kids of Ocracoke Village with stories of the ghosts and legends that haunted his island. The place was so full of spooks and specters that he could probably tell a story every day for a year and not repeat himself. And if he needed a little embellishment or a prop to sell the story, well, a bit of theatrics wouldn't hurt, would it? He had once told a story about how his uncle had killed a werewolf with a silver dollar. When the kids didn't believe him, Adam pulled the bloodstained coin from his pocket to prove it had happened. But for this story, he needed a little more help.

"Half," insisted his friend Laura Eden. "I know you're taking these kids."

"I'm not *taking* them," Adam answered, "They're paying for a story. I'm only getting a dollar each. And there's only like ten of them."

"Half," said Laura again. "I gotta do the hard part."

So Adam agreed. The payoff would just mean the kids would come back for more. And, to be honest, he liked telling the scary stories. This time he was going to tell them about Mad Mag, the crazy old lady who lived in Paddy's Hollow long ago, and who's ghost wanders the cemetery. Laura was supposed to dress up as Mad Mag and appear from the cemetery when it got dark.

The day turned to dusk, and Adam gathered the flock of kids from the neighborhood. Their parents weren't worried. There was nowhere to go in the village that the kids couldn't be found. Ocracoke was an island, after all. And all the parents had done the same things when they were younger, scaring the little ones with spooky ghost tales, or being scared themselves. It was a rite of passage for the younger O'cockers.

The sun was just setting over the sound, casting a warm light on Adam, but making the shadows of the old twisted live oaks reach out over the dirt roads, with fingerlike shadows reaching out to the kids feet. Adam saw them skipping over the shadows, and decided to play on it.

"Alright, settle down," he said matter-of-factly as they stopped at the entrance to the Howard family cemetery. "Here, sit down against the fence," a long low white picket fence encircled the Howard family graveyard. They didn't go in, because it was hallowed ground, and because he didn't want them to see Laura before she had a chance to scare them.

Once they were calm, Adam began his tale...

"Now, you all know the name Mad Mag, right?" Quiet nods answered. The kids were already rapt. "Well, I'm gonna tell you the whole story, and more...

"Before she was Mad Mag, she was the beautiful Margaret Eaton. She lived up in Maine, and never was there a more beautiful girl. She was only fifteen, but she was gorgeous. She could sing and play piano, dance like a grown-up, she was just everything a girl wanted to be at the time.

"Unfortunately she was also what John Simon Howard wanted, too. He was a sailing captain who went up to Maine on his boat to carry freight back and forth. When he saw poor little Margaret, he plotted right then and there to make her his. Some people say he charmed her with his mature ways, others say he just up and kidnapped her. She was only fifteen, which may have been close to an adult at the time, but he was *old*. It would be five years before he could even say he was twice her age. But John Sime got her on his ship, and on the way back down to North Carolina he married her, somehow."

The kids made the appropriate sounds of disgust at the beginning of the tale. Creepy old people and marriage were both taboo to the little ones.

"Once he got her back to Ocracoke, he put her into his home and the two made a life together. But Maggie just wasn't used to life here. Some people think that crazy ran in her family. Others say John Sime drove her mad by taking her from her home. All good reasons, but I'll tell you something most people don't know..."

The kids leaned in, silent, bated, waiting for the hook that Adam always had.

"Up in Maine, it was always cool, gloomy, cloudy, overcast. Margaret loved the cool soft light. Here, it got hot, sunny, bright. They say she was so beautiful that she never cast a shadow when she lived at her home. But here, she saw her shadow. It chased her every day. She thought she lost something when she left Maine, but then she gained this sticky darkness that was always attached to her, stuck to her feet from morning to night. It drove her mad." With that, Adam lifted his foot, showing how the lest vestiges of sunlight made his shadow stretch long over the kids, over the white fence now oranging in the sunset, and into the graves beyond. "Every shadow reached out to take something from her, and she slowly went from Margaret to Mad Mag."

The kids ooo'ed and ahhh'ed at the revelation. They played with their own shadows, teasing each other with ethereal fingers creeping on each other in the twilight. Adam let them play for a moment before carrying on.

"She went mad after that, yes, indeed. There was a time she caught a stray cat and boiled it up for supper, to feed her husband. Boy was he surprised to pull a cat out of the soup pot that evening. And she branded herself on the head with an iron once. When John Sime died, the locals here built her a shack to live in down in Paddy's Hollow." He pointed to the woody area near their school, "and she lived there for the rest of her days.

"She lived right on the path to walk to and from the church, and to get to the beach. It was so close to the path that people would walk right up onto her porch. That drove her crazy, I tell you. And you little kids," he foisted the blame on the ones in front of him, even though the children that did the misdeeds were old or dead now, "would run by her shack and bang on the walls at night to scare her. She'd come running out screaming, her hair all wild, yelling and shaking fist, cussing out the kids as they ran into the woods.

"But the two really weird things she did," Adam paused to make sure he had their attention. The sky was closer to purple than orange now. He had to time it right, "were these. She chopped off her toe with a meat cleaver. No one knows why; they just say 'cause she was mad. I think she was trying to chop off her shadow, though.

"But that's not even the weirdest part," Adam thought he heard, maybe just sensed, some motion in the graveyard. "When she was alone, when she was older, she took to standing in the graveyards at night, just stand there, in her long nightgown, her hair long and white, blowing in the ocean wind, all stiff and wild from salt, just like her. She'd stand there, talking to herself, in the evenings. If anyone came by they'd just whisper 'Mad Mag' and turn around. No one wanted to be near her when she stood out in the cemetery.

"Why, even now, late in the day, some say you can still see her ghost, standing in the cemetery of the family that took her from her home so long ago..."

And with that, Adam looked up, in mock horror, as a woman in white, her hair crazy from the wind, came silently down through the ancient and worn grave markers of the Howard family cemetery.

The kids turned, saw the near glowing specter of Mad Mag, Maggie Eaton Howard, in the flesh, possibly, and screamed in unison. It took a wonderful moment of terror as Adam watched, all twenty feet of all ten kids stuck rooted to the spot, unable to move or break the spell. Then one broke for it and ran, tearing down British Cemetery Road at a breakneck speed toward the relative safety of the village and home. The spell had been cast and then broken, and all the kids now found their footing, their worn Keds shoes slipping in the dusty gravel as they all took off for home.

Adam waited a heartbeat to get them all clear, then laughed at their torment. Laura had done a great job scaring them, and he turned to tell her so.

"Oh, man, that was great!" he laughed, his sides aching from the joy of the prank. "You look perfect! You earned your pay tonight." Adam reached into his pocket for the crinkled wad of dollar bills.

Laura still stood at the top of the cemetery, as she spoke, "You just keep those damn kids off my porch." And with that, she turned and disappeared into the darkness of the trees.

A chill shook Adam for a moment. He then realized he had been standing still for a minute in front of a very dark graveyard. He, too, forced his feet into movement, a more sedate shuffle meant for a teenager, as he ambled back to the village. He would find Laura and give her her pay after she got out of her costume, he guessed.

He walked past the few grave markers outside the cemetery, including Old Diver, the mysterious grave of a deep sea diver who was supposed to walk the streets at night in his helmet. Adam nodded at the grave, saying "Next time, old man."

Once he came to the intersection, a girl in a white dress and big white beach hat came running up to him. Laura was breathing heavily, "Sorry I'm late," she gasped, "Did I miss them?"

Adam stood, open mouthed and silent, staring at Laura, in a very good costume of Mad Mag, but looking nothing like the woman he had just seen in the cemetery.

"What?" It was all Laura could get out.

Adam looked at her, then felt the soft paper in his hands. Without a word, he handed her the entire stack, all ten dollars. Someone earned that money tonight, but it sure wasn't him.

Joe Sledge

A Less Equal Death

Old St. Paul's Church, Newton
1861

Sundays at St. Paul's Church were days when everyone was equal under the eyes of God. The little church served a congregation that reached far over the land to the west of the Catawba River. The building was created by one man, barely a man at the time, over the short span of six months. Henry Cline, only eighteen years old at the time, built the two story church out of hand hewn wood logs. The outside was simplicity itself. A simple square sided block, not even a steeple or marking distinguished it as a house of God. But the inside was truly made to allow all who entered to, for one day at least, fully express their religious piety. The inside was a glorious design of Cline's skill and devotion to God. With room for 250 people, all were welcome, all were equal to hear the word and come to pray.

It was just that some were more equal than others. And some were less.

Built in 1818, the church seating was designed for a different age. Children, girls, and women sat in separate pews than the men. The pews for the women were open in the back, allowing for space for the ladies' ample dresses and hoops. A foot bar allowed mothers to rest weary legs while holding a baby on their lap. The men received a more simple and straightforward pew.

Slaves were treated less well. Nominally allowed the same access, they had to traverse a narrow set of stairs to the steep and hot upper level of straight back wooden pews in a tiny balcony overlooking the preacher. While some slave owners might sit below in feigned confidence that they were in their benevolent right to allow their slaves in the same building, it was more likely that this just allowed them to have closer access and control over the enslaved people.

But if nothing else, the church seemed to be the safe place for everyone who came through the doors.

This was sadly spoiled on a hot day in 1861.

C. M. Hildebrand was only 25, but he had decided to take on the title of "Colonel." It sounded good, and as a young landowner of a goodly plot of land, he liked the way it made him feel important. He also liked to lord it over the people he enslaved. Hildebrand worked his land hard, and ruled with an iron fist over the enslaved men. He hated when they disobeyed him, and came down hard on any shows of defiance.

So when a man escaped from his plantation, Hildebrand hunted him down with rage and wrath.

Hildebrand set forth on his horse to track the man who escaped him, figuring the slave making a run for freedom would not get very far. There were no resources, no support, it was hot, and the slave would be afraid. The residents did little to help Hildebrand. They didn't like the cocky young man, easily prone to violence and braggadocio, but they also had no love lost on the enslaved people. And they wanted to keep Hildebrand at arm's length if they could. So they pointed and walked away when he asked for any information. Hildebrand didn't care. He just wanted his man.

The day drove on, hot and relentless, as Hildebrand finally closed in on the slave. Looking for any place to hide or provide shelter, the empty church with its unlocked doors, a place of worship, always open, seemed to be the only and last refuge for the escaping enslaved man. If he could avoid detection until dark, he might make his way to the Catawba River, the tall trees giving him shade, the water quenching him. But that was not to be. Hildebrand, hot and sweaty, covered in dust, tired and bitterly angry, tracked the man to the church.

The slave had tried to hide in the one place that promised some form of comfort, the church loft, where the enslaved gathered on Sunday mornings. Hildebrand entered the church and discovered the fleeing man, crouching at the bottom pews. Angry at his property, the way Hildebrand saw it, the "Colonel" drew his pistol instead of taking the man back to be imprisoned. Hildebrand pointed the large barrel and fired.

The deafening cough of the pistol rang in Hildebrand's ears, and echoed through the church, built so that all could hear the word of God. But this time, Hell had issued forth in the sound of the gunshot instead.

The defenseless man was stunned at first. The lead ball thrown by the black powder pistol was notoriously inaccurate, but also notoriously deadly. It took a moment for him to realize he was mortally wounded. He clutched at the gunshot, his hand drenched in blood. Staggering, hoping against hope to somehow still find a way to escape, he put his hand out to steady himself, then fell to the wooden floor with a last rasping breath, and died.

Hildebrand felt nothing as he dragged the body out. He had to return to his plantation and bury the body. He couldn't leave it in the church, he knew, and he wanted to send a message. It would take days for the news to travel through the land of what Hildebrand had done.

The next Sunday, as with all Sundays, the church doors would be open to parishioners to hear the Word. Women and children on the left, men on the right, and slaves above them all, staring at the bloodstains. When Hildebrand showed up for church, a leering smirk on his face, the parish got eerily quiet. No one wanted to sit with Hildebrand, of course. Everyone felt the glare from above.

As Hildebrand sat down in his usual pew near the back, and the other men made space so as not to touch the air he breathed, the organ began to play. The creaky old pump organ began a haunting melodious tune, unrecognizable as a hymn, but mesmerizing in its simple sound.

Only no person sat at the organ. As more and more people turned to see the organ play by itself, Hildebrand began to notice the attention turn from his entrance, to the organ.

And then back to him.

It had only started to play when he came in and sat down. The tune played on, decidedly rhythmic, but not spiritual. Or not godly, they were all sure. The sound had a soft squawk, an off pitch hint, that began to ache at the teeth and heads. Behind it was a murmur, a sound of hundreds of people in sotto voce judgement, whispers of hate. It was not music that belonged in the house of the Lord. It was a theme song of evil, a marching tune for Hildebrand and his brand of malevolence. As more and more people stared at him, Hildebrand felt the hairs on the back of his neck rise. It was a distinctly unpleasant feeling.

Hildebrand got up to leave, the music playing in time with his step. As he finally exited the church, the organ wound down in a low warble to nothingness.

Hildebrand found that when he passed by the church, even without going in, on any day or night, the organ would begin to play, and only stop as he got past and out of earshot. He would never enter the church again. Within a year, a bloodletting of another kind would occur, when the Civil War would rage across the country. HIldebrand first tried to use his power and money to buy his way out of service, hiring others to serve in his stead. Then he attempted to use his self proclaimed Colonel status as a recruiter. As more and more able bodied men were called to serve and die for the southern cause, Hildebrand tried more and more to escape the actual fighting.

And the truth was, no one wanted him. When he didn't have to worry about someone fighting back, Hildebrand was brave and cocky. But in reality, he was a coward who wouldn't fight when someone fought back.

He avoided most of the war, but couldn't avoid the sounds in his head. He began hearing the organ sounds, even when he wasn't near the church. A sickness ran in him that he was terrified to tell or seek help. As his mental health waned so did his physical health, and so went his farm with it. He had lost his plantation, his power, his enslaved people had been freed and long left, and now he lost his mind. On November 14, 1868, C.M. Hildebrand fell into a strange coma and died.

His madness having taken him, and the church members sufficiently comforted by his punishment in this world, and assured of his punishment in the next, they buried him in the acre reserved for the departed, next to the St. Paul's Church. A simple marker was placed at the grave. Within a few days, the parishioners noticed the marker had fallen, and went to place it upright. It fell again, and again, over the years, until it finally broke off its base. The church decided to leave it as it was, broken on the ground.

In the coming years and ever since, the ghostly organ can still be heard coming from the church. Even though the church is no longer used, as a new building was built to house the growing population in the 1950s, the old St. Paul's was still cared for and preserved. But no amount of cleaning could wash away the sin committed in the loft above. To this day, the blood stains still remain, soaked into the wood as a constant reminder of the death that took place on hallowed ground. And the organ still plays when people pass by. The tune is different, a sorrowful and wistful tune that mixes regret with a plea for forgiveness.

Joe Sledge

The Voice From The Ether

WCNC, Elizabeth City
2019

When I was a kid, my world was different. Bigger, and smaller, at the same time.

I lived in a beach house that was already old even though I was young. Everything was old, the plumbing, the fireplace, the beds, the smells, the sights and sounds. It was all wonderful and glorious. At night we would wander the house, seeing what each other was doing, going from the front porch where we counted cars, slowly, to the upstairs to listen to the radio where it came in better. At night, it was WCNC and Joe Lamb playing popular music of that time.

WCNC was this mix of all the new music and all the regular news of the day. Joe Lamb could make a bloodmobile drive at the mall in Elizabeth City sound exciting. He was an hour away, but for a little kid, that was as far as Zanzibar. WCNC was the other side of the world, but it was also part of home. Joe Lamb was always there, at his radio station, telling us about what was happening, turning his Rs into Ahs with his unique mix of the Mid-Atlantic radio voice and eastern North Carolina twang. He was that uncle that always had some wild story to tell. And we all listened.

But the Seventies turned into the Eighties, and radio changed to cassettes and CDs for teenagers, and Joe Lamb sold the station and it changed formats and it never was the same. And I changed, too. I went to college and got a degree, and came home and got married and had kids and everything was right with the world. Like anyone who gets older, I reminisced about my old stereo and the sounds of my records. Smart phones and playlists just aren't a big part of us old guys' lives. I'm sure somewhere in the world the words Hi-Fi and vinyl are still used. Just not with my kids. When I hooked up the old components to my stereo and saw the soft glow from the old receiver, it took me back to when I was a kid, staying up late, tuning in every station I could, writing them down, finding the interesting old shows and satellite broadcasts. I would hear Flashback, a national show, then I could pick up Little Walt, a DJ in Windsor that played gospel music from above the cleaners, with his everpresent signature, "Tell'em Little Walt... SENT'CHOO!"

So I was reminiscing when I found my list of stations I had made when I was a kid in middle school, and there on the paper, in my messy scrawl, was WCNC AM 1240. But when

I tuned it in, all I got was static. Not even dead air. The station was well and truly down, gone. Gone for good.

My job kept me traveling, which was fine with me. My kids were older and had lives of their own. They had little interest in their father's travel, which meant I could do as I pleased. So after a day of work up in Pasquotank County, I decided to drive to the old tower and station for WCNC and see if anything was even still there. The sun was low and going down as I drove through Elizabeth City toward the old station. The tower was out in the woods, in an old residential area, with a few houses nearby. The road was disused. Over the years, the place had been cared for, kept up, and at some time they had planted a line of trees down the road. Now they were full grown, wide, unkempt, big field trees that reached over the road and filtered the orange light of the late evening sunset. Early summer warmed the air, and twilight was playtime for the many insects that flew through the warm shadowy evening. As I drove up, out of nostalgia, I tuned the radio to the old AM signal. Curiously, I got a mix of static, and some sounds, broadcasts probably from Virginia mixing in with the old channel, no longer clear and tinny. Through the static, I recognized the mellow Seventies sound of England Dan and John Ford Coley singing *I'd Really Love To See You Tonight*. Mid-Seventies mellow gold wasn't really my thing; I was a product of the Eighties and New Wave, but being an adult now, the easy groove of the music I had heard in my childhood was a warm comfort. I smelled my beach house, hot, salty, driftwood, and suntan lotion. It wasn't really a bad thing.

The song faded out as I got closer to the station. Saddened, I started to turn down the volume to eliminate the static, when another song came on, this time clearer. I remembered the sound, not the band, and the song got to the chorus just in time to tell me the title, *Moonlight Feels Right*. "Southern belles are hell," I agreed to the nameless band. I let it play through the seemingly endless xylophone solo.

The radio station was as abandoned as I thought it would be. A light still gleamed from the tower, a necessity, but the station seemed abandoned. I shut the car off and got out.

As I started to walk toward the station, a nondescript pillbox of a building that described nothing of the slow jams and singalongs that had come out of there over decades, I saw an equally nondescript light flicker on over the entry door. That alone didn't surprise me; surely it was some sort of security light. The sun was near to setting, and my approach had triggered a sensor.

What threw me was as I got closer was when the door slowly creaked open.

Okay, maybe just a peek. I mean, I was invited.

When I stepped in I could see that the entire station was not entirely dark. The entry was completely empty. This was not what WKRP in Cincinnati looked like at all, I thought. My imagination was playing tricks on me. I was sure I heard the soft sounds of George Harrison's guitar from somewhere in the building. Soft lights came from a room down the hall. I guessed, or maybe tried to delude myself, that the station was a repeater for another one. But the signal should be coming in clear as can be. I found a speaker on the wall and switched it. Harrison's *My Sweet Lord* crinkled through the old pressed wood speaker case. The sound was old. Wonderfully old. Like what I used to hear as a kid, the flat sandpaper of AM radio, coming across the ether, like it had to work at it, to get all the way to the beach and my ears. For a moment, I was 8 years old and not scared of being in a nearly abandoned radio station.

Then I remembered I was not 8 years old, and in an empty radio station that was playing music from the past.

I kept hearing sounds, more than the eerie background of old music, like someone was nearby, in the dark. Soft footsteps, switches and clicks, the strange sliding sound, as if someone was pulling and filing LP records on a shelf. My curiosity overcame my fear and I moved deeper into the station, through the dark hall. I knew the DJ booth was nearby. There had to be someone in there, making these noises, still playing records. Maybe it was just someone having fun, broadcasting on a weak signal to the neighborhood.

As I got close I could see the window to the booth, with a mix of soft lights coming through the glass. A few stickers clung to the window, including a WCNC bumper sticker that I remembered seeing when I was 5 years old. But as I got closer and closer, the light faded, as did the music. By the time I got to look in the booth, the last song, vague, indistinct, unrecognizable except for the easy drone that told me it was old, the soft yacht rock of a lost time and a former generation. Even the static faded to nothing.

I looked in the window. The booth was empty, old and dusty. Two platters sat still on one side of the board. Dials were turned down. There wasn't even a microphone in the place. The radio station wasn't just dead. They had stripped the corpse. Even the shelves, the libraries that once held the vast supply of the easy going groove that had come out for decades were empty. Not even a single album, unloved and abandoned, sat on the shelves. Still curious, I opened the door.

The only lights came from a soft security lamp and a weakened Exit sign. I could tell without looking closely that nothing had been touched in years. It took a lot of imagination to see Joe Lamb, sitting in a comfortable rolling chair, spinning from place to place, consulting a clipboard or reading Billboard magazine, seeing what songs would come next. He would put an album down, line up the needle, and spin it back to get ready for the next song. I wondered how he would feel about today's digital music, all lined up, the entire day's tracks available and probably paid for already. He truly was from a different time. I knew he had passed away, but I wondered if he lived to see the station he built go silent.

But it wasn't entirely silent. When I got there, it still played. Someone, somehow, was playing music, what would have been the adult contemporary tracks from the Seventies, and would now be Golden Oldies, probably. Well, here's to you, I thought, spinning an empty turntable with a finger, whoever you are. Keep making that music.

As I turned to walk out, I noticed a slot in the door, and a thin pad of paper. They were request slips, little notes, before post-its ever came around, just strips printed and glued together. I picked up the pad, with the WCNC call letters, logo, and frequency. I wasn't one for souvenirs, and I didn't want to take things that weren't mine. But they were just left, left behind, from another time, before a request could be messaged in, or however they did it now, if stations even took requests any more.

Instead I pulled out my pen and wrote a note, my request, nothing special, I thought, not my favorite song, but just something appropriate. Then I felt foolish. I crumpled the note in my hand and walked out, closing the door behind me. "'Night, Joe," I said to the dead air.

I walked out quickly, making sure I closed the doors and left no mark of my visit. I felt I was visiting an abandoned grave, with the spirits of the family watching from a distance. Even the dingy light buzzed and went out as a walked away from the station.

I got in my car and started it up. It was time to go home. It was late, already dark, my wife would be looking for me already. Tomorrow would be a new morning.

I had forgotten that I had left the radio tuned to the open station of WCNC. It was just a soft background to my tires crunching over gravel and dirt. I was surprised when I heard the first sounds come from the speakers. Soft and quiet at first, but then I heard the words, and the music...

"This is Joe Lamb on WCNC AM 1240. This song goes out to our biggest fan..." And then the unmistakable tones of Gerry Rafferty and *Baker Street* came pouring through the speakers.

I looked at the paper I had taken, crumpled and folded. I didn't dare to open it back up.

The Plea From The Grave

Wilmington
March 1810

"I swear, that wife of mine will be the death of me."

Samuel Jocelyn would be right and wrong with his statement.

Samuel and his best friend Alexander Hostler sat together at a table outside Jocelyn's lodge at the edge of the great wooded swamps that bordered Wilmington. Wealthy enough to afford a life of leisure, a home in the port city as well as a lodge inland, Samuel would spend many days with his best friend Alexander, both hunting and discussing the curious points of life of which one could think when the day to day needs and wants didn't interfere with the lifestyle of the idle rich. Over the years, they had discussed many things, from the considerations of marriage to the possibility of life in the spirit world, of life after death, ghosts and hauntings.

Tonight would bring an end to those conversations, and a rather strange beginning to another one between the two. It would be much more horrific than either can imagine.

Samuel Jocelyn had been married less than a year. Being young and wealthy, it had not been difficult to attract a bride, and he had fallen happily for the beautiful Mary Ann Sampson. She was from another wealthy family, so there was no concern of money for either. It seemed a marriage made in heaven.

It would take less than a year to send them into hell.

The close quarters of winter had brought out the worst in Mary. She argued with Samuel. The woman seemed to be constantly walking a knife's edge of any argument. Samuel was disappointed and disillusioned. He felt like he loved Mary, at some time. But she became cross, and distant, even in the same house. He had hoped that Spring and the coming of brighter days would change her dour expression, but Mary showed no plans to let up. Samuel had come from yet another argument with her that night. An escape outside with his friend Alexander, a glass of port wine, and some good discussion would ease his mind some.

"I swear, that wife of mine will be the death of me," he said as he took a sip of his drink.

Alexander grimaced, open discomfort on his face, not so much for the conversation, but for the sadness in his friend's message. "Do you remember when we talked about life after death? Not spiritual life, but the idea of a spirit living on, a physical presence? Do you think that these are brought on by trauma, like yours?"

Samuel laughed, "Do you think that I want to remain here after I die? I may relish the passing, just to be out of her presence!"

"I am serious, Samuel!" insisted Alexander, "And I do not want to see you suffer with her. I do not want to see you pass on, either. I do wonder about what happens in the great beyond. Of all the mysteries, it is the one where we must go alone. Do you not wonder if there is a way to guide another, or communicate, or wonder about if we can remain behind when our bodies and spirits separate?"

"Certainly."

"Do you think a soul can communicate with the living across the ether? How would one do that? How would you test it?"

Samuel, oddly more calm now talking about death than his present life, and warmed by a different set of spirits, smiled at his best friend. "No one can know that, without taking the ultimate test, it would seem.

"I say this, let us make a pact. A promise. Yes, it is a journey we must make alone. One of us will pass before the other, that is likely. The time and date is unknown, but that much upon which we can count. When one of us moves on, if we can, we will try to communicate with the other over the distance."

Alexander found this discussion morbid, but heartwarmingly intimate. The best and dearest friends would call to one another, and listen, even after death. "But what shall we say? What will be the sign? Will we leave something that marks the presence of ourselves in the afterlife?"

"Who can tell?" Samuel yelled joyously. "Who among Man can define the world next to ours?! I can say only this, Alexander. You have been my closest and dearest friend. Stood by me through all my life. If there is one person I can trust, it is you. Surely you will know the sign I give to you, no matter how far it must travel!"

The two agreed, pouring yet another drink to warm themselves on that cool March night. Neither knew at the time how apropos the toast would be. On March 15, 1810, Samuel Jocelyn would go to bed slightly drunk, and definitely alone.

On the night of March 16, he would have another argument with Mary. This time, with the realization that he would be happier alone, he got on his horse and rode off into the night, into the depths of Honey Island and the swamps that surrounded the land. In his anger and haste, he would not take his cloak, riding off in only his meager jacket. In the dark, blinded by the cool wind and his own sadness, Samuel Jocelyn would wind through the mysterious swampland at night until he struck his head on a low and formidable branch. It knocked him from his horse, and the man fell into the cold shallow waters of the swamp, unconscious.

It would be two days before Samuel's body was found, still in the same place, waterlogged, damaged, and partially frozen, as well as most assuredly dead.

Bodies did not last long back in that time, and a hasty burial was a necessity, even if it didn't allow time to grieve.

Samuel Jocelyn's remains were buried in the cemetery of St. James Episcopal Church. While many mourned their loss, Mary notwithstanding, Alexander Hostler took it extremely hard. He had been there when Samuel was dealing with his marriage, but had no power to help his friend. And now he was dead, clearly and utterly lost to this realm. Alexander found little peace in trying to sleep. There was a darkened hole in his heart where his friend had been. While Alexander had no idea of the hereafter, he knew definitively that here, at this time, in this life, this world was a bit more empty. He found himself falling into an exhausted and fitful sleep.

The middle of the night brought only more anxiety and fear. Alexander was approached in a dreamlike state by his late friend Samuel with the plea to dig up his grave. "Why did you bury me when I am not yet dead?" pleaded the specter in his dream. Alexander woke up, still in the middle of the night, exhausted, his body like a beaten rope, but he was unable to find more rest. The morning came to a bleary eyed Alexander Hostler.

The next day, looking for comfort, he mentioned this dream to a close friend, Louis Toomer. Toomer at first put the nightmare to being caused by the shock of loss of his dear friend. Then he asked, "Do you consider it may have something to do with how you discussed life in the afterworld so frequently? Perhaps your mind plays tricks on you."

So the next night came, and sleep came better to Alexander. Until the dream came again. It felt so real, as if Samuel Jocelyn were standing right at the foot of Alexander's bed, as he pleaded, "Come dig me up! You have buried me when I am not yet dead!" Another restless day and evening would pass.

By the third night, Alexander dreaded sunset and time for sleep, but his body ached. When the dream came yet again, the next morning he went to find his friend Louis Toomer. Together, the two wondered if this was some way for Samuel to communicate from the afterlife, but what a strange and horrific message. The two men formed a secret and clandestine pact. That evening, after the sun set, they would go to St. James church and dig up Samuel Jocelyn's grave. Perhaps there would be a message, a sign meant for Alexander, from the other side.

As they crossed the threshold of the graveyard, the cool night air gave their chills a boost. It was already spooky and eerie where they were. They were doing something highly illegal, immoral, and terrible to their departed friend. But they had to, if only to ease the troubled hearts that still beat for the one that was silent.

The ground had not yet packed, and digging was easy. The two worked in silence in the bright waxing moonlight. They reached the coffin easily.

With no ceremony the two men set about to rip open the coffin lid. The coffin nails and fancy wood stood little chance against the desperation of two men. What they found was not the message from beyond the grave that they had hoped against hope. Instead it was a shock of pure terror that they discovered.

The remains of Samuel Jocelyn were not at eternal rest as they had thought, His body was spun over in the grave, twisted and disjointed. Samuel's eyes were open, but unseeing. They would never see again. The look on his face, already drying and beginning to peel from his skull, was one of pure terror. His hands were bent, his nails broken and ripped from the fingers. The underside of the coffin lid, once lined with the soft silk afforded to the wealthy as they passed, was ripped and pulled, then the hard wood was scratched and clawed to deep ruts.

In their haste, the family had buried Samuel alive.

His body, nearly frozen from the cold March nights, stuck unconscious in the shallow water, had brought on a kind of coma. Only when the body was allowed to warm slowly was Samuel able to regain his self awareness. He had awoken from his hibernation to a darkened box, too small to lift his legs or head. Realizing he had been buried alive, he struggled to escape, tearing at his casket until his body gave out. Only his mind remained, calling to his best friend across the ethereal plane, but his message had been misunderstood by poor Alexander.

Samuel Jocelyn died days after being buried alive.

Alexander Hostler would be distraught at the thought that he could have saved his friend. He wondered if there would ever be a message from beyond, the way they had planned. Would Samuel ever try to communicate, or was that bond lost forever?

Alexander would visit Samuel's grave, often to apologize or plead for forgiveness. In his distress, knowing that whatever punishment Alexander could give himself in atonement, it would never be the same as what poor Samuel went through.

Then one night, passing by the graveyard, Alexander slowed, as he often would, to think of Samuel. He began to think he could still hear Samuel Jocelyn calling out, from deep in the ground, calling and wailing to anyone to hear.

Long after even Alexander Hostler was dead, people still would hear the muffled moans of Samuel Jocelyn coming from the graveyard of St. James Church. Young people would dare their friends to go find the grave and lay on it, to listen. The challenge was to see if they could remain there for an hour, or fall asleep. The daring youth rarely lasted more than a few minutes before the muffled groaning pleas came late at night through the hallowed earth.

Even now, with the fences up to keep the ne'er-do-wells off of poor Samuel's grave, there still is activity in the graveyard. From outside the graves, even from the street, late at night when the air is still and cool, a passerby will listen and hear the call. Samuel is still trapped, unable to escape completely the realm where the dead and living mix. And on those late evenings, when the moon waxes and lights up enough to see deep into the graveyard, sometimes people see the figure of Samuel Jocelyn's ghost, a simple cloud of dark smoke, gliding across his grave, one more restless soul to wander the orchards of the dead.

The Witch of Brownrigg Mill

Edenton

There is nothing more beautiful than a glassy lake, thought the young fisherman as he walked up the dirt path to Dillard's Millpond. Especially when you can fish it alone.

Dillard's Millpond was a long thin lake that had been pinned in hundreds of years ago by an old mill and dam. Back in the 1700s it was known as Brownrigg Mill, but the place had changed hands so many times, no one really knew who descended into ownership. Probably the fishes, he thought as he found a shady spot, one of his favorites, to look over the smooth dark water that ran almost imperceptibly into the nearby Roanoke River. Where the Roanoke flowed like a steady freight train, Dillard's Mill was still as a teacup. Its tannic water flowed only if you looked closely, if you could only stay still long enough to stop and stare. The young man was bound and determined to do just that.

The stillness of the pond's surface was only an illusion. He knew the water ran deep, and flowed with purpose. It was rich with both shade and light, and there was plentiful opportunity for life to take hold. Fish and other wildlife thrived there, and he planned to catch what he could, a big lunker bass or just hook a carp or crappie. He didn't care. He just enjoyed being outside, alone, with the long dark lake out in front of him.

The lake was a mix of shining glass water and beautiful ancient trees with roots planted into the soft loamy mud. Far out to the west, still in deep shade, stood the oldest of the cypress and pines that grew along the pond edge. Long ago the legends told that the dark forest held evil spooks and ghosts. Men feared to tread there, and worried what they may find. The pond was rumored to be unimaginably deep, even bottomless, and in its darkened depths it held secrets that none wanted to know.

He shivered in secret delight at the thought of people being afraid of his fishing spot. He didn't go over to the other side of the lake because it was thick, buggy, and difficult. Fishing would be just as good here, he said to himself, because there was no one else to talk to.

Casting his line, trying out a weighted spinner first, he just enjoyed the glint of early sun on his lure, and the diamond ripples it made when it splashed. He looked over at the berm, repaired now after a hurricane wiped it out years ago. The mill and old dam were long gone.

After about thirty minutes, he began to hear the small sounds of life along the pond. Sitting still, nature became accustomed to him, and he knew that the wildlife, not really that wild, would show up. He had seen squirrels, rabbits, deer, sometimes a raccoon at dusk, plenty of birds, and the occasional wandering dog or cat loose from a nearby neighborhood. But other people were a rare sight. So he was a little surprised when an old man walked up on him. The fisherman didn't even hear his footfalls until the old man was right upon him.

"Any luck?" he asked, the usual singsong question asked to all fishermen for hundreds of years.

Startled, but with a kneejerk reaction, the young fisherman responded, "Not yet. Day's young," he pointed over his shoulder at the early morning sun. The implication was clear. What are you doing out here this early? Why are you interrupting my fishing?

The old man took no mind of the hint. "You're lucky, anyway. Being able to get out here, on your own, no one to stop you. You married?"

"No," said the fisherman. "I'm only 19," he thought to himself.

"See? Lucky." said the old man. "I've been married. Twice. Neither worked out. Now I get to be out here all the time.

"You ever wonder what happened to the old mill and dam over there?" the old man seemed to change his subjects really quickly.

"Sure, I know," said the fisherman, "it got knocked down by Hurricane Matthew, back in 2016. They rebuilt the berm," he pointed to the long stone wall, "Fishing was terrible there."

"No," the old man said as he shook his head, "the real mill, the original one."

The fisherman put down his pole. Nothing was biting anyway. He might as well hear the old man's story, then maybe he would get some peace and quiet. "Well, you must know. So tell me..."

Back in the 1700s, the pond was known as Brownrigg Mill. It had a watermill powered by the pond, and it made flour and meal for the local towns all around the river. It was run by a kind, burly man named Tim Farrow, a widower with a young daughter. He was well liked by the other people of the area, a good father, as best as he could be considering his circumstances, and ran his mill with efficiency. He wasn't used to things changing, or surprises.

One day he got a surprise as a boat appeared in a cove near the river. As he went to see it, a pile of rags and cloth moved inside. Farrow discovered that in the small boat was a beautiful, striking young woman. He was stunned by how charming, almost perfect, she was. Her eyes glistened like gold, sparkling like the water did on a summer evening. As he helped her up from the boat, she explained, "I was traveling down the river with my husband, but we were lost in a storm. He died a week ago up in the Virginia colony. I have traveled so far and long. Is there any place I may stay for the night and get some food to eat?"

Farrow, struck by how beautiful the woman was, offered his home. "I have an extra room, and plenty of food. Please stay with us for the night. You are perfectly welcome to stay and rest as long as you need."

The woman smiled, white teeth shining, her face beaming with the invitation. "Thank you so much," she said as she accepted the invitation.

So she stayed the night.

Then a few more nights.

After a few weeks, when the traveling minister came through, she and Tim were married.

It seemed idyllic, at first. She kept the mill and house clean, cooked, and helped care for the property. Tim was beyond happy. The rough, burly man that ran the hard workings of the mill found a softness when he came home to his bride. His days passed more easily when he looked forward to the evenings.

But after a while, his life took small dark turns. His neighbors seemed jealous of him, having a new and beguiling bride. One neighbor mentioned how, when the woman spent a night at their house while Tim was away, that the bed she used barely looked slept in. Only a small impression at the foot of the bed showed any markings of use. Quiet murmurs occurred in the near towns and villages, and fewer people came to the mill.

Tim noticed that his daughter, still young at age six, had an aversion to the woman, bordering on panic and terror.

Every time Tim's wife would go to touch the girl, to stroke her hair, Tim's daughter drew back in fear. She never let the woman go near her. Within weeks, the girl would go to live with family in Edenton.

The mill began to have problems, too. Farrow found sacks of meal, scratched and torn. The mill wheels, normally smooth, nestled tightly to grind flour to a fine powder, now scraped and sparked. Tim was finding nails hidden in the wheels, throwing off the millworks and ruining the flour.

And then there were the cats.

A stray cat around a mill was generally a good thing. It meant that the mice that invariably show up would stand little chance against a prowling hunter. But Tim noticed there was more than one in the nearby woods. Two, or occasionally three, would appear, and Tim saw that they weren't always the same ones. There were cats of different colors, wandering the woods, coming from the dark forest to the west, but never getting near him.

Around that time, Tim noticed a change in his wife. She no longer worked around the house. She slept most of the day. Only when he came home and fed her did she wake up, passionate and aggressive, full of life. During the day, she slept, curled up tight on a small love seat.

With all that was happening, all the signs, and even though Tim Farrow didn't want to believe it, many of his neighbors were now saying out loud that his wife was a witch.

The accusations only isolated him further. But he could no longer take not knowing why all the strange things were happening to him and his mill. He liked order and simplicity. The chaos of his life was more than he could stand.

One evening, he stated he was going into the nearby town for several hours. He walked down the dusty road, the sun setting over his shoulder, until the shadows of the trees reached out to his feet. Once dark enough, he ducked into the woods and ran back to his mill. He climbed up into the workings of the mill and hid. He had armed himself with an ax, sharpened to a glistening razor's edge. And he waited.

He didn't have to wait long. Within a few minutes of the sun setting, with just the dusky twilight of orange and purple filtering through the cracks of the mill, Tim heard the skitter of small animals. A strange chittering of talk, not human, but unlike any woodland creature he had heard before, came from the steps outside. Then the door began to rattle. Then shake. Then pound, as if heavy sticks bent to beat the door in.

From his hiding point, Tim watched with terror. The door flew open, crashing on its hinges, and a clowder of cats screeched in. There were so many, ten, twelve, fifteen, he couldn't count them as they scurried around the mill. They tore into the bags of flour and corn meal, spilling the contents out. They tore at the strings holding the bags with long and sharp white fangs. Their chitters of talk turned into a horrific high pitched laughter. The cats were enjoying the destruction they caused.

Tim, now more angered than scared, stood, ax gleaming through the dust flying in the mill. He strode forward, now back to the strong burly man he once was. In the distance, lightning flashed from an approaching thunderstorm. It only gave a greater menace to the scene before the thunder shook the mill.

The cats stopped, frozen, at first. Then, seemingly as one, began to approach and encircle Tim. He stomped his large foot, a promise to do damage to the cats for their damage done to him. But instead of running, the cats hissed and attacked. They scratched at his ankles, legs, and hands. He saw them in a blur as they tore through the mill. They stayed clear of his ax, which he swung wildly. He tried to cut at them or bash them with the blunt end, but rarely made even a brushing contact.

The cats were more severe in their attack. Each scratch was like a knife wound. His legs began to bleed. Painful welts formed on his arms and hands where they bit or dug in their claws. Tim realized if he didn't do something, he could possibly bleed to death. He saw one cat, strikingly orange, flaming fur, sleek and deceptively beautiful, as it perched on a high beam. The cat hissed a ferocious call, then jumped at Tim's face.

In a flash, Tim swung his ax to protect himself from the lunging wild cat. The blade flew through the darkening room, lit often by the oncoming storm's lightning. As he struck, so did the thunder shake. The ax found the front paw of the cat, severing it cleanly.

The cats screamed in pain and terror, as one. All felt the same pain, and all began to run out of the mill. Weakened and scared, Tim stopped to catch his breath. He surveyed his wounds. They were deep and painful. There was much more damage to him than he would suspect even a large number of cats could do. He moved slowly to the door. He needed to get to his house, home, for treatment and rest. He needed the care of his wife to treat his wounds.

Tim Farrow stumbled back to his house as the rain hit hard in sheets. What started as a darkening rainstorm had turned into a torrential downpour. The water overflowed the race of the mill's lock and poured down the wheel. The dam was pounded by waves of heavy water from upstream. Tim struggled to open the door to his home to get to the relative safety and dryness within.

He called for his wife, but she did not answer. He wound his way to their bedroom, where he found her. She was curled up on the bed, as was her usual posture. But this time, her dress and the bed were covered in deep crimson of blood. She looked up at him, her face a rictus of pain. Then, Tim saw through the pain to the look of anger. She grimaced at him, a look of hate in her eyes, as she rose from the bed, holding her arm.

It was neatly severed, just below the wrist.

Shocked into stillness, Tim's feet were frozen to the spot. He watched in horror as his wife transformed into a cat, one paw missing, still dripping blood, as it hopped and staggered out of the room and into the storm outside.

Tim was petrified by the sight of his wife turning into a cat, blood covering their bed, and the realization of all that had happened. They were right; his wife had been a witch. She brought her coven to his home, run his family and friends away, and nearly killed him. So distraught, he never heard the sound of rushing water until it was too late.

The dam gave way, flooding the home and mill. Tim Farrow was swept away, into the depths of the millpond. He drowned in the same waters that he had called home for all those years.

The old man paused for a moment, just to let the story set. The young fisherman, once nonplussed at hearing a bit of useless history, now sat quiet and intrigued. The old man told a good tale. For all he knew, it could very well be true. Well, maybe not the part about the cat.

As if reading the young fisherman's mind, the old man went on. "Some fishermen, like you," he nodded and pointed, "found Tim Farrow's body days later, far over on the other side of the lake," He pointed to the dark trees to the west.

"When they found him, he was all beaten and bruised from the storm, and cut up from the cats. But the really strange thing, when they pulled him out, he had clenched in his tight fist the paw of a cat."

The old man chuckled as he walked away. "Mark my words, boy. Marriage... it's a real commitment. Careful who you catch out of this lake. Careful who you feed." And with those words, he drifted down the path and disappeared.

The words of the old man hung in the air around him as the fisherman cast his line, mechanically, without thought or joy. After a few tries, he felt the soft tug on the line. He waited, then set the hook and reeled in a small fish. It was a smallmouth bass, not big enough to keep. As it wiggled, impaled on the barbed hook, out of the corner of his eye the fisherman saw a glint of movement. A stray cat stood, impassive, proud, on its haunches. A soft and silent pink tongue licked in hope and anticipation. He looked at the cat, finding himself trying to count its paws. Then he stared at his catch, too small for him, but a decent meal for a hungry stray. The words of the old man came back to him.

He unhooked the fish and tossed it back in.

"Nope. This one's not for you, kitty."

Joe Sledge

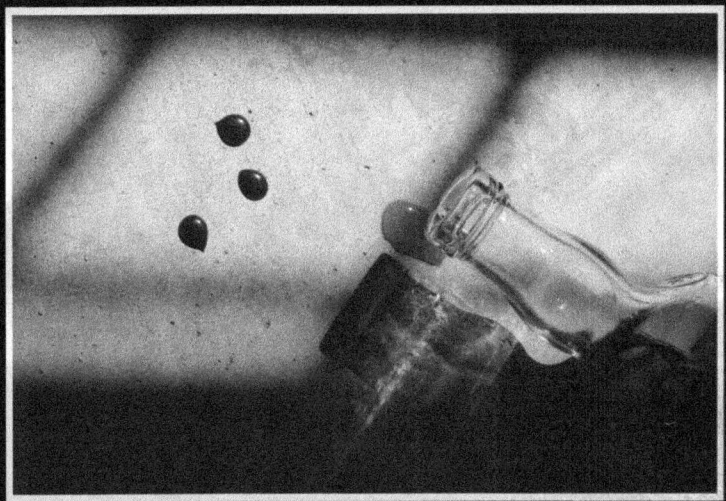

Chicken Alley

Asheville
1902

Alone or in small clusters, dark shapes trudged their way through the city streets to a darkened alley, one of many in the city of Asheville. The shapes were vaguely men, intent on reaching Broadway Tavern and the drunken revelry that hid behind its closed door. The door cracks open, just long enough to spill light out onto the alleyway, and let the shapes in. Broadway Tavern was popular with the loggers and lumberjacks of the area, who came to Asheville for jobs with pay good enough to afford cheap liquor and easy women. Alcohol and disease flowed freely enough that many of the men would need treatment or care for insult or injury. Fights were common, almost predictable.

Luckily there was a doctor in the house.

Late at night, heading down the darkened streets, came the familiar *tap tap tap* of a cane rapping on the stone alley. Attached to the cane was one of the vague dark shapes, only this time the figure, though fully hidden, was most easily recognizable. The long black duster, wide brimmed hat, and the onyx black cane were all sure signs that this was Dr. Jamie Smith. He was headed to the Broadway Tavern, and he certainly was making no house call. It was nighttime, and Dr. Smith aimed to have a good time.

He was a man of means. A good doctor, well practiced at his craft, he was well to do. His cane, black with a silver wolf head handle, showed he was successful. His black bag, worn and frayed, showed he worked hard. His desire for a drink meant he was done with work. When Dr. Smith showed up, a good time was going to be had. Sure as taxes. Sure as death.

This night, hell would follow Dr. Smith into the tavern, and the wounds would be too much for the doctor to fix.

As he entered, the lumberjacks had already started their drinking and fighting. A scuffle busted out on the floor. Tables, already broken or damaged, of little use except to lean upon, were overturned, chairs scattered to the corners to make better use of the open spaces for brawling. The fight took seconds to move from a scuffle to a brawl to a melee. Dr. Smith, not wanting a fight to ruin his drinking, waded into the battle, his silver tipped cane raised high to bring down on some poor logger's skull. Any damage he did, he could surely make right again the following morning. Or afternoon, depending upon when he or the victim awoke.

The mob fought itself, never finding any actual target. They just wanted to fight. But drunks feel less pain when lubricated and anesthetized. They also make worse decisions. Unable to determine the difference between friend and foe, one brawler did not see the sympathetic doctor who treated their diseases and cuts. He only saw an easy target, the back of a man in black. A knife was drawn and plunged into Dr. Smith, through his back and fully into his heart. Blood flowed freely on the dirty floor. The tavern was salted with Dr. Smith's blood, as he laid on the ground, an unceremonious death as he passed away on the floor of the Broadway Tavern.

There was an investigation, of course. Everyone was shocked at his murder. But the loggers kept quiet. As gruesome as the murder was, no one told on one of their own. The murderer was never caught. The Broadway Tavern lost much of its luster, not that it had much to begin with. But the crowd was more subdued. No one liked to walk the floor where poor Dr. Smith had passed. They tried to clean the blood, but the crimson marks remained. As the crowds would file out, less rambunctious, more sad at being drunk now, and more quiet, sometimes they heard things. The bartenders, too, late at night, once people had left.

Tap tap tap...

The sound of Dr. Jamie Smith's cane was still heard walking the streets, and the alley of the Broadway Tavern. Men still visited the dirty watering hole, but drank to hide the memory of Dr. Smith, and when they heard the sound, *tap tap tap*, they were reminded of who they had killed, and who they let get away.

Within a year the Broadway tavern went from lively and raucous to dark and dreary. Then, one night, mysteriously, it burnt down. The fire consumed it utterly, burning the place to ash.

Asheville continued to grow, and the land was cleared and buildings went up in place of the old tavern. The alley became a place for residents to buy chickens that were slaughtered nearby. It was still a sanguine location, but at least there was less human blood shed. Still, the proprietors would notice that if they stayed too long and the sky got dark, somewhere, hidden in the darkness, they heard it, the *tap tap tap* of Dr. Smith's cane as it walks across the alley. Even today, where the alley has become part of apartments, the residents say they still hear it, late at night, as the ghost of Dr. Jamie Smith walks the alley. Occasionally, someone will leave out a drink, a simple shot of cheap whiskey, to find the glass still there in the morning, upside down and empty. Dr. Smith is still looking for one more drink.

The Thing at the Alligator River Bridge

Dare County

Wind and rain lashed at the windows of the bridge tender's lookout. Johnny Blivens stared out the window and he was only able to see a few feet as the rain blurred out the river to the south and north. Lights shone on the two passages under the swing bridge. He could see the rain blowing sideways under him. No boat was coming through tonight, he thought. Any sailor worth their salt was in a marina or at least on a hook in a protected part of the river tonight. To put an exclamation point to his thought, the storm threw a dull rattling splash of rain against the tower.

Johnny stretched in the tiny bridgetender's building, a thick, industrial block of concrete that would easily withstand the storm outside, just as it had withstood hurricanes since 1962, when the bridge was completed. He looked across the bridge, which ranged from Tyrrell and Dare counties to the west and east. Seeing no cars, he ducked down to the small head and kitchenette below. There were no windows on the downstairs room. It gave him a bit of protection from the noise of the storms, as well as needed privacy. He carried his portable VHF radio with him, but, like he had said to himself, no one was going to be out on the river looking for passage this night.

He had just flushed the toilet when he heard the familiar *skkrrt* of his radio getting a call.

"Bridge tender.... this is *sckkkk...* ing vessel *chhhkk... tude* requesting open passage..."

"Really?" thought Johnny, "It's after midnight, in a storm, and you call before I can get my hands washed." Johnny knew the boat out there had no idea what he was doing in the tower, and couldn't be blamed. But still...

Johnny washed his hands. The boat could wait that long. They hadn't even followed proper procedure, hailing three times first, and they hadn't identified themselves by name or vessel. He grabbed a bottle of water and a bag of vegetables from the refrigerator. His daughter had been pushing him to eat healthy since his job was sedentary. Johnny knew he was supposed to be a tubby old coot sailor, but he loved his daughter with all his heart, and did whatever he could to please her. If staying healthy for her and her near due baby, his grandchild, would make her happy, well, carrots and water it was.

Up on the lookout, he tried to find the boat, where ever this fool was. "Vessel, repeat your hail. Make sure you say your vessel type and name, okay? Are you sure you can make the passage?" He looked at the wind speed. It was well below the 35 knot wind limit for opening the bridge, but the wind, rain, and darkness always made a tricky pass through the old bridge.

"Bridgetender, bridgetender,... bridgetender," Johnny wondered if this sailor was counting on his fingers, but he got the first part of the hail right, "This is... *skkkrrrt...* motor sailboat *Longitude* requesting an open passage."

Johnny picked up his binoculars, not that they would do much good. He looked north, then south, but saw no lights except the channel markers in the water. "*Longitude,* which direction are you coming from? Which way are you going? Do you have lights on? I can't see you. You need to be running lights out in this storm, buddy."

"Bridgetender.... Motor sailing vessel *Longitude* requesting passage from south to north." With those words, a dull greenish white light came on. It looked low in the water, almost shining out from under the blue green water of the Alligator River. It was like this fellow was learning to operate his boat as he was going along.

Okay, so it's going to be one of those nights, Johnny thought. "Hold on a minute," he said. Johnny wanted to make sure there were no late night drivers out. There was no need to hold up a lone car for this one. Seeing no lights through the wind and rain, he began the steps to open the bridge.

Before he could do anything else, he needed to get the red lights on and the gates down. It was an easy, well practiced, but incremental set of steps to open the bridge, and if he did it wrong, he'd have to start over. Johnny definitely didn't want to spend more time than needed with the bridge open in the storm. So, the lights came on, the gates came down, and the red glow blinked, rhythmically, through the waves of an early summer rainstorm. Of course, as soon as the bridge began to open, Johnny saw the unmistakable lights of a long 18-wheeler rolling through toward the Outer Banks. He watched the truck roll slowly to a stop at the barrier. The amber lights on this one trailed long across the trailer. He liked the ones that were well lit, colorful. He figured the owners took good care of their rides. Johnny liked to guess what was on the big rigs as they found their way to the barrier islands. If they were labeled, the trucks had their brands, a grocery store or a gas station, it was easier. But someone had to deliver the beach towels, discount sunscreen, nekkid lady bottle openers, all the junk that tourists just had to have to make their vacation better. Right up until the time they threw it all away at the end of the week.

Johnny guessed this one hauled...

A huge gust of wind shook the tender house, lashing it with dirty translucent waves of water. The truck shook from the wind, then began to move. The wind buffeted the side of the big semi, picking it up from one side. The whole trailer began to tilt. In the red glare of the lights, Johnny saw the wheels start to lift.

The truck driver jumped from the cab and ran toward the leeward shelter of the bridge tender's tower. Johnny saw him and ran down to him, opening the door and letting the poor shaken man in from out in the suddenly strengthening storm.

"I..." he stammered, "I thought I was gonna go over!"

"You're okay now, buddy," Johnny consoled the man. He looked out, seeing the truck still shake from the storm, but staying put on the bridge deck. "You're truck's okay there, too."

"Yeah, sheesh, good thing you opened the bridge when you did. If I had been passing over at speed..." he just shuddered without finishing his sentence.

Johnny didn't need him to. He had seen two trucks tip over in high winds on the bridge, one time killing a man. He didn't want to see another.

"Bridgetender, *Longitude* commencing passage..."

Johnny was shook from the reverie of the fortunate truck driver coming to a stop on the bridge. Johnny realized he took his eyes off the boat with this novice skipper for too long. He returned to his post to see it as it would pass through the far opening.

When he looked, he couldn't see much. It wasn't just because of the wind and rain, but because there wasn't a boat out there. A strange black shape cruised through the water, glowing greenish white lights, that looked more like... eyes?

He tried to look closer, through his binoculars, but the rain blotted out his view. As it passed through, the lights dimmed and disappeared into the night. Johnny watched, stunned at what he just saw. Or didn't see.

"Thanks, bridgetender. *Longitude* is clear.

"Tell that truck driver to take it easy the rest of the way."

With that, the voice faded into the silence of the static on the ether.

Summer came in earnest in the coming days. Johnny said nothing about what had happened to him that night. He dutifully recorded the name of the vessel with a note that he couldn't get the vessel number due to weather, and hoped no one ever said anything about it again. And he kept trying to ignore the lights he saw appearing in the water late at night, swimming around the remnants of the old maritime forest over on the Dare County side. And he really, really tried to ignore the lights he saw when they occasionally came up under the center of the bridge, just under the big swing span.

The problem he had was that whatever it was, it didn't want to be ignored.

At first, it was just the calls. Johnny would get a hail, a clear one coming through the VHF, and an obvious boat asking for an open passage due to their tall air draft. As he would be opening the bridge, he would hear it, coming through the ether. "Bridgetender, this is *Longitude*, requesting passage..." And there, behind the real honest to goodness regular everyday sailboat was a real honest to goodness regular, but not every day, thankfully, river monster. The sailors passing through never even noticed it behind them.

Then it asked him a question. "Bridgetender, Bridgetender..."

"... This is the bridgetender... go ahead..."

"... what's your name?"

Really? This thing wanted Johnny's name? He didn't know how to answer. The sailing vessels and motor boats that came through regularly would ask his name and then call him by it. This was a bit of professional courtesy, and a sign of respect. Now, it sounded creepy. He didn't know what to do. Ignore it, give a fake name? He always told the boats that passed by his name if they asked.

"It's Johnny."

"... Hi, Johnny..."

And that was it.

By the middle of June, Johnny gave up on his diet and started eating potato chips. He needed something crunchy to worry about in his mouth. He added some weights to lift and did stretches out on the deck when no one was watching. Then he realized that someone or some thing probably was watching. He had to do something to keep his mind from wandering to the sea monster down below him. His daughter had made him promise not to get fat while sitting alone at this job. Yeah, he thought to himself, worry is gonna keep me thin.

One evening there was a line of boats stacked up. Johnny held them in the calm water for as long as he could to let the summer traffic full of minivans and big pickups hauling campers down to Hatteras through and not stack the cars up to Columbia or East Lake. He finally found a momentary opening in the traffic and started the bridge procedure. Lights on, wait for them to stop, gates down, begin opening.

Whenever this happened, invariably people got out of their cars and walked to the side of the bridge to watch the boats pass through. They would pose for selfies, throw footballs, and try to plaster one more sticker on the Draw Bridge sign. With the long fifth wheel trailers behind the trucks, and the darkness of twilight, no one else saw what Johnny saw. Up from underneath the bridge, an amorphous blob would crawl across the wooden trestles and under the bridge span, then up and over the side of the bridge. Johnny would watch, unsure and somewhat terrified, as the thing began to creep toward the nearest truck, a big shiny Chevrolet pulling a ubiquitous trailer, along with a huge cooler, bikes strapped to the back, fishing poles jutting out, just waiting to be broken. The first time he saw the thing, Johnny watched, in terror, until he saw it reach into the big storage bin in the back and pull out a crinkly, shining yellow bag. Then, with a dexterity meant for only gymnasts, it slipped back over the side of the rail into the water.

He looked at the space where the thing had been, then down at his own hands, still greasy, as he wiped them on his shirt. It had stolen some tourist's bag of potato chips.

Other weird things happened, too. A couple of fellows in a sailboat they just bought were sailing down the Alligator River when the motor went out in a storm. They couldn't make passage through the bridge, and tried to sail into the marina next to it, but the wind was just too strong. They ended up throwing out the hook and anchoring as best they could. In the middle of the night, it looked like they would be dragged into the bridge, but when they woke up the next morning, the boat was anchored just offshore, upwind from where they had been the night before.

A motor boat out scooting around the river, cutting through the spans, ended up with its propeller fouled by a big hunk of rope. Even on the calm evening, they didn't have as much luck as the sailors did.

And one night, Johnny got the hail. "Bridgetender, Bridgetender, Bridgetender, *Longitude* requesting open passage."

Johnny, cringing, looked out into the clear starlit night. He knew what he would see. Nothing. Nothing at all. He got on his radio and responded, "I can't do that." He almost pleaded with the thing. "You know I can't."

The lights came on in the river, bright and clear, from the south. "*Longitude*, requesting passage."

Johnny just couldn't do it. There were heavy fines involved with opening the bridge unless it was needed.

"... Open the bridge, Johnny..."

The tone, the insistence, and the vague threat. Johnny didn't like being threatened, but he also didn't like the idea of that thing crawling up to his tower in the middle of the night. To add to it, the lights shone a little more brightly.

Johnny gave in. He turned the lights on, lowered the gates, and began the opening. As the bridge swung out, he saw approaching lights from the mainland side, moving fast. They met the bridge and began the mesmerizing blinking they did as they shone through the sides of the bridge's retaining rails. Johnny could always tell how fast someone was going by how fast the lights blinked. This one was a blur.

Then Johnny saw more lights behind it. Blue rollers of the local Highway Patrol. "When those party lights are on, buddy, the party's over." The kid in the pickup slowed, caught on the bridge. Unable to turn around, and unable to go forward, he was dead meat, thought Johnny. He watched as the kid got hauled out of the big pickup. He must have been really flyin', thought Johnny, for them to take him away like that. If he hadn't had the bridge open...

"Bridgetender, this is *Longitude*. We are clear. Thank you for passage."

Johnny wrote it down in his log as he waved to the troopers down below. And never said another word about it.

Johnny did everything he could to keep the thing at the Alligator River Bridge out of his mind, but little helped. He could see the places along the bridge that had strange thin scratches where it had climbed up in the night. It didn't matter if there was a full moon or the sky was dark and overcast, he still saw it, slipping up on the deck, looking around, occasionally peering at a truck or RV stopped on the bridge. Johnny was just happy it never showed up at his tower. At least, he never saw it at is tower.

He did a little research of what had been seen in the river. This thing certainly was no alligator. They rarely appeared there anyway. The closest he could find was a grindylow, which was a strange freshwater mermaid, he guessed, that looked like a giant tadpole, but with webbed arms and legs, eyes the size of saucers, and big long claws that would stretch up out of the water to snatch little children. They were legends told in old England to keep the kids away from the water's edge, he figured. We never did that, he thought to himself. We practically threw our kids in the water. He thought of his upcoming grandchild, how her life would be shaped by living on an island over in Manteo. He looked forward to spending more time with her. Maybe give up this job, go ahead and retire.

Johnny made his weekly pilgrimage to the grocery store to pick up snacks for the small galley below his lookout. He grabbed a bag of potato chips, and the memories came back to him, of the thing, the grindylow, sneaking over the side of the bridge to steal food from the tourists' vehicles. He wondered how many little kids the thing had startled or scared. How many parents would shush them for telling lies? Johnny grabbed a couple extra.

That night, he put out two bags of chips on the rail. The night was calm, starlit, with just a bit of good waxing moon out to shine on the rippling water of the Alligator River. Only one boat passed through, soon after he took over his shift. The rest of the night was quiet. The next morning, only one bag of chips was on the rail.

The week went by wonderfully for Johnny. Nice evenings fell into dull and beautiful nights. No strange noises over the radio, no weird shapes on the bridge decking, no lights in the water that weren't supposed to be there. By Friday, he began to wonder if it was all over. Maybe the thing found somewhere else to go. Maybe he imagined it. He didn't know, and didn't care.

Then, Johnny spied a boat coming from the North, out of the deep black of the night. Through his binoculars, Johnny could see the unmistakable bi-colored lights, a bright masthead, and even the glow of the stern light. At least it was just a regular sailboat. He waited to see if they would put in for the evening or ask for passage.

"Bridge tender, bridge tender, bridge tender..." there was a heartbeat of pause as the radio squawked, "This is sailing vessel *Tiki Torch* requesting an opening for passage under power, over."

These guys are pros, Johnny recognized, the singsong lilt of a sailor skilled to the point of bragging that they were making the exact right call over the radio, even punching the call button late at night to add a little squeal just in case the tender was asleep. Alright, he thought, you're good guys, I'll get you through. He opened his radio and began to speak, "Sailing vessel *Tiki Torch*, hold at the marker for opening. You are out late, *Tiki*. Are you okay for sailing?"

"Aye, Alligator, we want to make Ocracoke by sunrise. We're good and safe." He meant they were sober, Johnny knew.

"Alright, *Tiki*, just checking. Hold for opening." And he clicked off the microphone.

No sooner had he reached to turn on the red lights than the familiar crackle came over the radio. "Bridgetender, ...*skkk*... leave the bridge closed. *Longitude* hailing. Leave the bridge closed to boat traffic."

Ugh.

Johnny thought he was free of his river monster. That it was all a dream.

"*Longitude*, I can't do that. I have to open for passage. There's nothing coming."

...

"Leave the bridge closed, Johnny."

The way it said it. It wasn't really a threat. But it kind of was. It was like an assurance. Like something bad would happen. The thing had opened the bridge before. To stop a truck from blowing over, and to stop a crazy speeder. But there was just nothing, no reason.

"... Johnny..."

Okay.

"Sailing vessel *Tiki Torch*, hold for a minute. We, uh, may have need for the bridge." He didn't know what else to say.

"Aye, Alligator," was all the response he got, but their tone was really one of them not liking to be disappointed.

Then he saw the headlights. A car was racing from Tyrrell county toward the bridge. He was going pretty fast, fast enough that if the Highway Patrol spotted him, they wouldn't like it, but probably not so fast that he'd end up in jail. The car looked like it was on a mission, Johnny guessed. He watched as it reached the bridge, its lights doing the same blinking that all fast cars do as they fly along the span. The car quickly made it up to and past the opening, then sped off into the night. "Lucky him," Johnny thought. "I just saved that guy a half an hour, probably."

121

"Okay, Johnny, open the bridge."

Yeah, yeah, the bridge. Okay... "*Tiki Torch*, Alligator River Bridge is opening." He went through the routine, watched *Tiki Torch*, an excruciatingly beautiful sailboat of blue and white motor through, handled by an immensely handsome man, decked out in perfect sailing garb, flanked by equally an perfect woman and teenage boy, presumably a family, pass through, and then radio in the same singsong voice, "Bridge tender, we are clear. Have a great night."

"You, too, *Tiki*." And Johnny waved, while breathing a very deep sigh of relief.

The calm lasted a moment before his cell phone rang. "Mr. Blivens? This is Jody, your daughter's friend? She wanted me to call you to tell you she started labor just now."

"Is she alright?!" Johnny looked around, unsure of what to do, stuck so far away in a room growing smaller by the second.

"Yes, she's fine," reassured Jody. "She just wanted me to call you. We called her husband first. He's coming back from Rocky Mount tonight, and we were just going to say if you see him to leave the bridge closed for him, you know."

"Okay," Johnny went numb. "...Okay... I'll, I'll um, try to get someone here to take my place tonight, but it will be a while. I'll get there."

It had taken an excruciating hour to get someone to come spell Johnny, but he had finally been able to head to the beach and the hospital where his new baby granddaughter waited for him. Mom and Dad were exhausted but happy, over the moon at the healthy little girl. His son-in-law patted

Johnny on the back. "I was so worried when I came over the bridge. I saw that sailboat there. If you had opened the bridge, I wouldn't have made it in time. The baby's days early and I would have been half an hour late. Thanks, Mr. Blivens."

The next evening, as Johnny settled in to another dark night, he set a bag of potato chips on the ledge. Soon after, he heard the familiar staticky call.

"Bridgetender..."

"Go ahead, *Longitude*."

"... Thanks for the chips.

"I like the crab flavored ones."

Joe Sledge

Afterword

I don't know what to say.

I just read this, as any author does, to check for errors, get a feel for the stories, see what needs to be changed. And, wow, I loved it. I'm not trying to brag. I'm a pretty humble guy, really. Yes, I'm proud of the work I did in this book, but more than that, these are great stories. I was entertained by my own work.

That's not an easy thing for a writer to do.

Even after writing this, I wonder why ghost stories are so appealing. Not in the sense of why would someone like ghost stories, but what is it about these spooky tales that make them so entertaining, what draws us to them with a near addiction. I know we like them, but why do we like them.

There's the bloodthirsty appeal, the ability to read something that scares us, and then go to sleep, to prove we can handle it, the hot sauce of literary works.

And they represent a promise of a tie to the past and a promise to the future, that things go on, past the times we can comprehend. A ghost is proof of an afterlife, even in a story.

But there is more to it. The scares and joys are visceral, deeply internal, something that meets a need inside of us that can't be defined, and probably shouldn't be. I think they go into the needs of all of us who must have something beyond the simplistic, the surface. This is why the stories are important, as are the storytellers. Life does best when there is more to it than just another day older and closer to death. Stories fulfill us, even when we don't realize it. We need the singers, songwriters, poets, writers, movie makers, all the creators, just as much as we need the day to day mundane tasks. We just don't always notice it.

Kind of like our ghosts.

They walk the land, hidden in shadow, eclipsed by the light of day to day actions, where most of us don't see them. They go unnoticed, until we call out, until we looks sideways, until we think for a moment about the footsteps that went before us in this land. This Haunted Land, its history and how it ties itself to our present and future, shape us just as we bend the land to our will. Twist too hard, and our future will be bent. Stop and listen, see what the ghosts might be saying. They know where the treasure is.

About The Author

Joe Sledge is the author of four books in the Did You See That? series, a collection of roadside attractions across North Carolina, with the coordinates of each location included. Joe has also written two books of ghost tales, this book, and Haunting The Outer Banks, Thirteen Tales Of Terror From The North Carolina Coast. Additionally, Joe penned two works of fiction. Bess Truly And Her Zap-Gun Rangers is a book written for his daughter which is equal parts Nancy Drew and Radar Men From The Moon. Under the pen name John Martell, Joe wrote The Unmerciful Sea, a horror novel that takes place in Ocracoke. He also edited and annotated Nag's Head; Or, Two Months Among The Bankers, first written in 1850 about vacation life on the Outer Banks.

Joe is a graduate of UNC Chapel Hill and an avid traveler. When not writing, he and his family spend as much time as possible traveling throughout North Carolina and beyond. In addition to writing, Joe runs Gravity Well Books, his publishing company.

Joe Sledge

Photo Credits

All photos by Joe Sledge, unless otherwise noted. All photos are under copyright of their owners, and are used with permission. Copyright of photos is extended from the initial copyright at the beginning of this book. No duplication or use is allowed without consent of the owners of the photos. Photos are used for entertainment purposes only, and may not be the actual location of the tale.

Introduction Trees - Chris Updegrave
Lake Cammack - Lee Capps
Church Pews - Marjorie Kaufman
creativecommons.org/licenses/by-sa/4.0/deed.en
Chambers Hall, Davidson University - Public Domain